Isaac William

Hymns translated from the Parisian breviary

Isaac William

Hymns translated from the Parisian breviary

ISBN/EAN: 9783741192807

Manufactured in Europe, USA, Canada, Australia, Japa

Cover: Foto ©Andreas Hilbeck / pixelio.de

Manufactured and distributed by brebook publishing software
(www.brebook.com)

Isaac William

Hymns translated from the Parisian breviary

PREFACE.

NATURAL piety would turn our attention to the ancient Latin Hymns, as the source from which our acknowledged deficiency in Metrical Psalmody is to be supplied. And indeed our Church itself points out to us these fountains, and leads us, as it were, by the hand to them; inasmuch, as in the same books of devotion we find most parts of our own Prayer-book. Moreover, that which may be accounted the only metrical Psalm, or Hymn, fully authorized by the Church of England, viz. the *Veni Creator*, inserted in the Ordination services, is one of these hymns. And perhaps the reason why more of them were not introduced into the Prayer-book, was rather the difficulty of finding persons competent to translate them at the time, than any other cause. Archbishop Cranmer did himself attempt it, at least the " *salve festa dies*," as he mentions in a letter to the king, expressing a desire, that as his " English verses wanted the grace and faculty which he could wish they had, his Majesty would cause some other to do them in more pleasant English and phrase [a]." At any rate, though nothing is more opposed to the wishes of the translator than that any of these Hymns should find unauthorized admission into any of our Churches, yet, so far as they have preserved the character of the original, they are much more congenial to the spirit of our own Liturgy than those Hymns which are too often made to take part in our ancient Services.

With regard to the mode of translation, it was first intended to have had the Latin printed together with these Hymns, in the manner that they have occasionally appeared in the British Magazine; by which it would have been seen how far the originals have been closely adhered to, which has been done for the most part; and how far, as in other cases, the liberty has been taken freely to paraphrase rather than to translate. The chief reason for not thus printing the Latin Hymns has been, that they are to be procured in a small edition, recently published at Oxford, which comprises mostly the same which are here selected. Some of them are in the original not free from objection, such as those on the Eucharist, on the Blessed Virgin Mary, and on the Remains of the Dead; but it is hoped that there is nothing whatever in these translations but what is perfectly agreeable to the doctrines of our own Church.

The subjects of these Hymns, and the allusions which they contain, are frequently such as cannot be understood without some knowledge of the Breviary Services, which it would be too long a work, and foreign to the present intention, to explain; as, for instance, the Hymns for the different days of the week not only contain allusions to the work of the Creation on those days, but also, with reference to it, a particular key-note, or lesson appropriate to the day. On the first day love to God and His commandments is inculcated; on the second, God's love to man is the subject; on the three following days, Faith, Hope, and Love; on Friday, the patient virtues and the sufferings of Christ; on Saturday, thanksgiving for those who are with God, and rest from their labours. In like manner not only have the Festivals, but their Octaves also, a peculiar and appropriate topic: for instance, that of the Epiphany, is the Baptism of Christ; that of the Ascension, Christ's return to Judgment; that of All Saints' Day, the mortal remains of the dead. This circumstance has prevented the Hymns from being adapted, as could have been wished, more strictly to our own Festivals.

The Hymns on the days of St. Stephen, St. John, and the Presentation, have been supplied by a friend.

Oxford,
The Feast of St. John the Baptist, 1839.

CONTENTS.

HYMNS FOR THE WEEK.

HYMNS FOR THE SEASONS.

PERSONS AND EVENTS RECORDED IN HOLY SCRIPTURE.

COMMEMORATION OF SAINTS.

HYMNS FOR THE WEEK.

The Lord's Day.

AT MIDNIGHT.

Die dierum principe.

MORN of morn and day of days,
Silent as the morning's rays,
From the sepulchre's dark prison,
Christ the light of lights hath risen.
He commanded, and His word
Death and the dread chaos heard :
We, O shame, more deaf than they,
In the chains of darkness stay.
Nature 'neath the shadow lies;
Let the sons of light arise,
All throughout night's stillness deep
Holy symphonies to keep.
While the dead world sleeps around,
Let the sacred temples sound ;
Law and prophet and blest psalm,
Lit with holy light so calm.

B

Thus to hearts in slumber weak
Let the heavenly trumpet speak;
And, like streaks of early morn,
New ways mark the newly born.
Grant us this, and with us be,
Sole fountain of all charity,
Thou who dost the Spirit give,
Bidding the dead letters live.
Equal praise to Father, Son,
And to Thee, the Holy One,
By whose quickening breath divine
Our dull spirits burn and shine.

AT THE MATTINS.

"Hear, O Israel: The Lord our God is one Lord: and thou shalt love the Lord thy God with all thine heart, and with all thy soul, and with all thy might; and these words shall be in thine heart: and thou shalt talk of them when thou sittest in thine house, and when thou walkest by the way, and when thou liest down, and when thou risest up."—*Deut. vi.*

Ad templa nos rursus vocat.

MORNING lifts her dewy veil,
  With new-born blessings crown'd,
Let us haste her light to hail
  In courts of holy ground.

Christ hath shed a fairer morn,
  From darkness rising free,
In His glorious light new-born,
  Let us lift the jubilee.

From the swaddling bands of night
  When sprang the world so fair,
Putting on her robes of light,
  O what a power was there!

When our God who gave His Son,
  His guilty foes to spare,
Woke to life the guiltless One,
  O what a love was there!

When from the Eternal's hand
  The earth in beauty stood,
Deck'd in light at His command,
  He saw and call'd it good.

Yet a goodlier world it stood
  In the Creator's sight,
In the Lamb's all-cleansing blood
  Wash'd to celestial white.

In the light of rising morn,
  Which o'er creation flies,
We descry, by fancy borne,
  Heaven's courts beyond the skies.

In the image of the Eternal,
  In Christ, of souls the sun,
Dimly, through the fleshly veil,
  We see the Holy One.

In Thy law, bless'd Trinity,
 *A torch-light sure and true,
What Thou forbiddest may we flee,
What Thou dost bid, pursue.

Through the Week.

AT THE FIRST HOUR.

"Ye were sometimes darkness, but now are ye light in the Lord: walk as children of light: for the fruit of the Spirit is in all goodness and righteousness and truth; proving what is acceptable unto the Lord."—Ephes. v.

Jam lucis orto sidere.

Now morn's star hath woke from sleep,
 Let us at His footstool pray
That He would our pathway keep,
 Light unborn, our better day:
That hand or tongue this day do nought of ill,
Nor aught of vanity the bosom fill;
  Truth calm and free
  On our lips be,
And in our heart's throne sit meek Charity.

While this day shall onward roll,
 From the cruel foe's dark hate
Keep the sentry of our soul,
 Of our senses keep the gate.

That this day's service to Thy praise may be,
And as it is begun, so end in Thee;
  Nor pride unwind
  The treacherous mind,
But self-control the rebel spirit bind.

Oh, let us die from this world's vanity,
With Thee to rise, and treasure have on high;
  Singing of Thee,
  The eternal Three,
Still singing of Thee everlastingly.

Through the Week.

AT THE THIRD HOUR.

" Hereby we do know that we know Him, if we keep His commandments. He that saith, I know Him, and keepeth not His commandments, is a liar, and the truth is not in Him. But whoso keepeth His word, in him verily is the love of God perfected."—1 John ii.

O fons amoris Spiritus.

O SPIRIT, fount of love,
  Unlock Thy temple door,
  And on our spirits pour
Thy day-spring from above.

O Thou of the great Three,
  Who art the Union,
  Unite us all in one,
In bonds of charity.

Glory to God on high,
　And Him that cometh down
　Poor fallen man to own,
And Spirit ever nigh.

Through the Week.

AT THE SIXTH HOUR.

"This is the love of God, that we keep His commandments :
and His commandments are not grievous."—1 John v.

Jam solis excelsum jubar.

THE sun is soaring high,
　And wide from east to west
　Opens his golden vest,
And fiery panoply.

True Sun, who in the soul
　Liftest Thy torch unseen,
　Charity's light within,
Our better day unrol.

Glory to God on high,
　And Him that cometh down
　Poor fallen man to own,
And Spirit ever nigh.

Through the Week.

AT THE NINTH HOUR.

"The end of the commandment is charity out of a pure
heart, and of a good conscience, and of faith unfeigned."
1 Tim. i.

Labente jam solis rotâ.

Now the day's declining wheel
    Doth to night's dim caverns roll;
Thus hours, days, and seasons steal,
    Life is hurrying to the goal.
While Thou, with outstretch'd arms, bleeding
      and bare,
Art calling to a world that will not hear;
      Calling from high,
      Still ever nigh;
Hid in Thy sheltering arms, O let me die!

Oh, let us die from this world's vanity,
With Thee to rise, and treasure have on high,
      Singing of Thee,
      The eternal Three,
Still singing of Thee everlastingly.

AT THE VESPERS.

"Blessed be the God and Father of our Lord Jesus Christ, who hath blessed us with all spiritual blessings in heavenly places in Christ: according as He hath chosen us in Him before the foundation of the world, that we should be holy and without blame before Him in love."—*Ephes.* I.

O luce qui mortalibus.

O THOU who in the light dost dwell,
To mortal unapproachable,
Where angels veil them from Thy rays,
    And tremble as they gaze :—
While us the deeps of darkness bar,
From Thy bless'd presence set afar,
Till brightness of th' eternal day
    Shall chase the gloom away.

Such day Thou hast in store with Thee,
Hid in Thy boundless majesty,
Of which the sun, in glorious trim,
    Is but a shadow dim.
Why lingers thus light's golden wheel
Which shall to us that day reveal?
But we must cast this flesh aside
    Ere we with Thee abide.

But when the soul shall take her wing
From out her dark enveloping,—

To see Thee, praise Thee, love Thee still,
   Her urn within shall fill.
Dread Three in one, mould us, and ble ss,
In Thine o'erflowing bounteousness,
To pass unharm'd through this our night,
   And see Thine endless light.

AT THE COMPLINE.

"Ye are all the children of light, and the children of the day : we are not of the night, nor of darkness ; therefore let us not sleep, as do others ; but let us watch and be sober."—1 Thess. v.

Grates peracto jam die.

AND now the day is past and gone,
   Holy God, we bow to Thee,
Again as nightly shades come on,
   To Thy sheltering side we flee.

For all the ills this day hath done,
   Let our bitter sorrow plead,
And keep us from the wicked one,
   When ourselves we cannot heed.

Ravening he prowls Thy fold around,
   In his watchful circuitings :
Father, this night let us be found
   'Neath the shadow of Thy wings.

O when shall that Thy day have come,
  Day ne'er sinking to the west;
That country and that holy home,
  Where no foe shall break our rest.

Now to the Father and the Son
  We our feeble voice would raise,
With Holy Spirit join'd in One,
  And from age to age would praise.

The Second Day.

AT MIDNIGHT.

" He spreadeth out the heavens like a curtain, and layeth the beams of His chambers in the waters, and maketh the clouds His chariot."—*Psalm* civ.

Dei canamus gloriam.

GLORY to God on high,
Upon this day unfolding
  His tent along the sky,
To wondering man beholding.

Heaven's roof becomes a bed,
Where liquid lakes are pending,
  On earth beneath outspread,
In dewy drops descending.

An image of the dower
Thou hast for us prepared,
  Of grace the living shower
For them Thy love hath spared.

They drink that holy dew,
In faithful heart concealing;
  It heavenward springs anew,
Itself in strength revealing.

Blest people, on whose land
Such high gifts are pouring,
    Thy love and bounteous hand,
With fruits of love restoring.

Then let us Thy great Name
Day by day be singing,
    Till with the glad acclaim
Eternity is ringing.

AT THE MATTINS.

"I love them that love Me; and those that seek Me early
shall find Me."—Prov. viii.

Nil laudibus nostris eges.

Our praise Thou need'st not, but Thy love,
    Our Father and our Friend,
Would have our prayers thus soar above,
    In blessings to descend.

Thy secret judgments' depths profound
    Still sings the silent night,
The day, upon his golden round,
    Thy pity infinite.

The soul lost in astonishment
    Would speechless wonder fill,
But in the ravish'd bosom pent,
    Love cannot all be still.

Feeble and faint she fain would tell
  Of our great Father's love,
Tempering the ills that with us dwell,
  And pledging good above.

Thither would our best thoughts aspire,
  But chains on us abide ;
O quicken Thou our faint desire,
  And to Thy presence guide.

AT THE VESPERS.

"Whom having not seen, ye love; in whom, though now ye
see Him not, yet believing, ye rejoice with joy unspeakable
and full of glory: receiving the end of your faith, even the
salvation of your souls."—1 *Peter* i.

Jactamur heu, quot fluctibus.

Now us with winds and waves at war
The world's dark deluge bears afar,
There shines in heaven one lonely star ;
Thither we lift our longing eyes,
  And thither send our sighs.

A Father's help doth intervene,
  And from on high a Hand is seen,
The o'erflowing water-floods between ;
Man's weakness grasps with trembling hold,
  And grasping it grows bold.

What ills conspire, and work our fear,
But Thou than they are mightier ;—
The soul shall feel Thee standing near,
And lean on Thee the only good
    To burst her servitude.

And this vile body Thou shalt change,
To be like Thine own Son's, to range
O'er the wide heavens, expanding strange ;
But that immortal crown is won
    By pain and toil alone.

Bless'd pain and toil, whose short-lived state
A change so glorious doth await,
And joys no thought can estimate :
Who would not bear the short-lived pain
    Immortal bliss to gain !

To Him above, to Him below,
To Him, as was, and as is now,
To Him while endless ages flow,
To Father, Son, and Spirit raise
    All glory, love, and praise.

The Third Day.

AT MIDNIGHT.

"The sea is His, and He made it, and His hands prepared
the dry land."—*Psalm* xcv.

Jubes et in præceps aquis.

THE word is given,—and waters flow,
  And to the heavenly gale,
The earth uplifts her from below,
  And folds her humid sail.

Here hast Thou, Lord, Thy children set
  To dwell in one abode :
May they be here together met
  In holy brotherhood.

A brotherhood of exiles here,
  But to His house above
Are gathered by a Father's care,
  Who learn a brother's love.

Who hurt their neighbour with ill tongue,
  Or arts of evil leaven,
Thou puttest far from Thee, from song,
  And palace-hall of Heaven.

Lo, earth herself in agony
  The wicked scarce sustains,
And yearns in travail to be free
  From dark corruption's chains.

And we, too, in our spirits groan,
  And full adoption wait,
We, with the earnest of the Son
  E'en now predestinate.

Be endless praise, and aye remain,
  To God, both One and Three,
From whom in lowly hearts doth reign
  Fraternal charity.

AT THE MATTINS.

" A new commandment I write unto you, which thing is true
in Him and in you: because the darkness is past, and the true
light now shineth. He that saith he is in the light, and hateth
his brother, is in darkness even until now. He that loveth his
 brother abideth in the light, and there is none occasion of
stumbling in him."—1 John ii.

Te principem summo, Deus.

Thou first and chief dost, Lord, demand
  Our love to thee above,
And next to Thee, Thou dost command
  That we our neighbour love :
Look down on Thine own Church below,
Which in Thy love would live and grow.

Though many members, we are one,
  One body, heart, and soul,
And faith and truth together run,
  And fill the mighty whole;
But envy sets us thence afar,
And strife that wakes internal war.

The God of peace, a Father's care
  Such bonds must form and keep,
That we our brethren's joys may share,
  And weep with them that weep;
Then may His praises never cease
Who builds us in His house of peace.

AT THE VESPERS.

"Whether one member suffer, all the members suffer with it;
or one member be honoured, all the members rejoice with it.
Now ye are the body of Christ, and members in particular."
1 *Cor.* xii.

O quam juvat fratres, Deus.

How sweet it is to see
Brethren in unity,
The body, through whose veins
Christ's lowly spirit reigns,
Which lives and moves in Him alone.

How sweet one voice to raise
All in one house of praise,
Besieging heaven's high tower
With prayer's assailing power—
Sweet force, whereby e'en God is won.

Be it from Thee above
That holy house to love ;
Be peace for ever there,
And nothing e'er draw near
That shall disturb that union.

Woe unto such ! but they
Who love Thee and obey,
Shall find earth's trials rude,
Turn to their during good,
While foes but aid and help them on.

Far worse fell flattery's tongue,
In soft persuasion strong,
Which, with its pleasing wiles,
Its willing prey beguiles,
And makes the thoughtless heart its own.

Grant us, blest Trinity,
The love which flows from Thee,
That we on this our road
May bear each other's load,
And reign together round Thy throne.

The Fourth Day.

AT MIDNIGHT.

Miramur, O Deus, tuæ.

O God, we behold how Thy wondrous might
Hath hung with new works the vast infinite,
How, writ by Thy hand, 'mid the glimmering
    stars,
It shineth from far in strange characters.

The sun builds the day for his chamber bright,
The white moon sits on the throne of night,
While the stars all around like her army ap-
    pear,
And through the blue dark marshal here and
    there.

The sun, though he walks the broad heavens
    alone,
Knows his rising well and his going down;
The moon and her host they come and they go,
And silent and still to Thine ordering bow.

On the noiseless wheel of a whirlwind borne,
They carry away and they bring the morn;
These changes amid that around Thee dwell,
Thou art alone the Unchangeable.

Then why should the soul like a wave be
    driven,
If her anchor rests on the depth of Heaven?
If she make Thee here her healing and health,
She shall have in Thee her eternal wealth.

Great God, at whose will o'er the silent heart
The sunshine or shade do come or depart,
All glory to Thee: in Thee we repose,
And leave on Thy breast our sadness and woes.

AT THE MATTINS.

"In the way of Thy judgments, O Lord, have we waited for Thee; the desire of our soul is to Thy name, and to the remembrance of Thee. With my soul have I desired Thee in the night; yea, with my spirit within me will I seek Thee early."—Isa. xxvi.

Promittis, et servas datam.

THY promise, Lord, is our sure stay,
    Thy faith immoveable,
To Thee we turn at dawning day,
    To Thee our wants we tell.

Man's promise in the hour of need
    Frail as himself is found,
Which fails, and like the broken reed,
    The leaning hand doth wound.

Blessed is he who in thy breast
  Himself doth wholly hide,
No whirlwind's power shall break their rest
  Who in that Rock abide.

Lest our hearts fail, Thy hand shall hold
  With sacramental ties;
Hope on the mighty pledge made bold
  To endless good shall rise—

Springs to Thy throne on mercy's gleam,
  And casts aside her care,
And drinks of the celestial stream
  Which flows for ever there.

Of grace, adorèd Trinity,
  The everlasting spring,
Sole hope of safety, unto Thee
  With our whole heart we cling.

AT THE VESPERS.

"The God of hope fill you with all joy and peace in believing,
that ye may abound in hope, through the power of the Holy
Ghost."—*Rom.* xv.

Horres superbos, nec tuam.

Thou dost, Lord, abhor the proud ;
To the arrogant and loud
Thou hast ne'er the praise allow'd
    Which is Thine alone.

Thankless souls that will not pray
Turn Thy gracious stream away,
And like wither'd grass decay
    'Neath the scorching noon.

As the servant's earnest gaze
Keeps his master's hand and ways,
So our eyes we ever raise
    To Thy Sion's throne.

And shouldst Thou the gift withhold,
Yet to Thee the full heart told,
Hope shall on her anchor hold,
    And await the boon.

Glory be to God on high,
To the Son who came to die,
To the Spirit ever nigh,
    Sealing us His own.

The Fifth Day.

AT MIDNIGHT.

Iisdem creati fluctibus.

The fish in wave, and bird on wing,
From self-same waters spring,
And both in death their being give
That man may live.

The soul doth other food require,
Born of celestial fire,
The Word her sustenance, and Faith
Her vital breath.

From blood of Christ that Faith had birth,
And then went forth on earth,
And hath the nations, with kind sway,
Taught to obey.

It is a light in spirits clear,
   Which brings the calm heavens near,
And kindles into glorious deeds
    Eternal seeds.

Through faith the saints have lions quell'd,
   And kings by wrath impell'd,
And welcom'd with a peaceful smile
    The blazing pile.

Grant, Lord, that we the path may tread
   Whereon this light is shed ;
And gather fruits of love that throng
    That path along.

To God the Father be all praise,
   To God the Son always,
And God the Spirit we adore
    For evermore.

AT THE MATTINS.

"Ye are a chosen generation, a royal priesthood, an holy nation, a peculiar people; that ye should shew forth the praises of Him who hath called you out of darkness into His marvellous light."—1 *Pet.* ii.

Dignus quis, O Deus, tibi.

LORD, who worthy songs of praise
   Shall unto Thee repay ?
Scattering darkness with Thy rays,
   Thou shew'st salvation's way.

Faith which doth from Thee proceed,
To Thy blest courts shall lead,
Shall bid the soul's delusions fly,
And raise our hearts on high.

If Thy Spirit be not there,
No holy rite is sweet;
Secret hearts to Thee might bear
A sacrifice more meet;
Voice with heart, in union true,
Shall pay her tribute due,
And from the mouth, for utterance freed,
Shall saving truth proceed.

Thou dost hate the haughty brow,
Simple souls dost love :
Grant Thy faith in us may grow,
Swelling thoughts remove.
Praise to God in earth and Heaven,
And to the Son be given,
Who built His Church on His own blood,
And Spirit ever good.

AT THE VESPERS.

"With the heart man believeth unto righteousness; and with the mouth confession is made unto salvation. For the Scripture saith, Whosoever believeth on Him shall not be ashamed. For there is no difference between the Jew and the Greek : for the same Lord over all is rich unto all that call upon Him."
—*Rom.* 2.

O fortis, O clemens Deus.

MERCIFUL and mighty Lord,
Author of the saving Word,
Unto us Thy faith afford.

Keep the germ in us alive,
Whence we all our strength derive,
'Mid serener skies to thrive.

Arms, and shield invincible,
In whose shelter guarded well,
We the fiery darts may quell.

Hence our prayers to Thee addrest,
In that Name for ever blest,
'Neath whose shadow we find rest.

Let that Name reach Thee on high,
Hear, and help us when we cry,
Lest our lives that faith deny.

Father, Spirit, Son Divine,
Lit by Thee, as in a shrine,
Faith in the inmost heart doth shine.

The Sixth Day.

AT MIDNIGHT.

"Thou makest him to have dominion of the works of Thy hands : and Thou hast put all things in subjection under his feet."—*Psalm* viii.

Jam sanctius moves opus.

Now a holier work, O Lord,
  Thou dost move,
Taking counsel with the Word
  Of Thy love,
Of the new-born world a King,
And a Priest Thyself to sing.

Man is made, lit with the light
  Of Thy breath,
He doth walk with day and night
  Free from death,
And beneath the vaulted air,
Doth his Maker's image bear.

Where the bays of beauteous sea
  Range around,
Earth with rock and mount and tree
  Doth abound,
He shall reign a monarch true,
Paying Thee allegiance due.

Ah, how blind the reckless soul
 Set on ill,
This one yoke the sole control
 On his will;
Haughty dust doth nothing dread
E'en to God to lift his head.

Hence how great the dismal band
 Of our woes,
While the world on either hand
 Doth us close;
Christ, unless Thou bear us aid
Hope from guilty souls must fade!

Unto God who did us make
 Low we bow,
To the Son who for our sake
 Bore all woe,
And to Spirit from above,
By whose breath we live and move.

AT THE MATTINS.

"O Lord, be gracious unto us; we have waited for Thee: be
Thou their arm every morning, our salvation also in the time
of trouble."—*Isaiah* xxxiii.

Ultricibus nos undique.

WHILE Thine avenging arrows fall
 On every side,
Unto what mountains shall we call?
Where but in Thee for shelter hide?

The busy world with all her skill
   Can nothing bring,
Her remedies foment the ill,
And but augment the secret sting.

But from Thy scourges which we fear
   Our hopes arise,
The ills a Father bids us bear
Are of our wounds the remedies.

On our heart's lusts that rage and swell
   Lay Thou the rein,
These the worst ills that with us dwell,
The ills Thou only canst restrain.

Why tarriest Thou ? without—within—
   There gathers war
To try the soul Christ died to win ;—
Shall the great foe His conquest mar ?

Our prayers are heard,—the heart that
 grieves
   Again is strong ;
Thy death alone can, Lord, relieve
The fears that on our dying throng.

Glory to God above the skies,
   Who thus doth prove,
And those most dear with chastening tries,
But in His wrath remembers love.

AT THE VESPERS.

"Let us lay aside every weight, and the sin which doth so
easily beset us, and let us run with patience the race that is
set before us, looking unto Jesus the Author and Finisher of
our faith; who for the joy that was set before Him endured the
cross, despising the shame."—*Heb.* xii.

Lugete, pacis Angeli.

ANGELS of peace, look down from Heaven and
　　mourn,
　Lo, your own God low to the earth is bent;
Wearing guilt's image, of His glories shorn,
　Of wicked men He bears the punishment.

O miracle stupendous of vast love!
　O deadness of man's heart that still remains!
To die for you your God comes from above;
　Ye will not walk with Him and share His
　　pains.

It is Thy Cross alone, alone thy Cross,
　From everlasting flames our souls sets free;
Chasten us with fire, sword, or worldly loss,
　But spare us for a long eternity.

The flesh shrinks back, but 'tis His Father's
　　will,
　He bows His head and drinks the bitter
　　cup,—
In this Thy strength may we Thy law fulfil,
　Take from Thy hand the chalice, and look up.

Heal'd by the stripes which Thy pure body
          stain,
  Wash'd by the blood which floweth from
          Thy side,
Leave us not, lest we sin, and fall again,
  And thus another Cross for Thee provide.

Glory to Him, who gave His Son to die;
  Glory to Him, who for the guilty dies;
Glory to Him, who came down from on high
  To sanctify the holy sacrifice.

The Seventh Day.

AT MIDNIGHT.

Tandem peractis, O Deus.

AND now Thy labours, Lord, are done,
And on the sixth returning sun
Thou to Thy work hast set the bound,—
The Heavens take up the gladsome sound.

But while the Sabbath now is blest,
And consecrate to endless rest,
Another labour doth demand
The great Creator's mighty hand.

For all things now have found a tongue,
Together raise one rival song,
Together, earth, and sea, and stars ;—
One sinner the glad concert mars.

Our heart of stone, Lord, from us take,
And fleshly hearts within us make,
That so abounding fruits of love
A welcome hymn to Thee may prove.

Such are the hymns which Thee delight,
The deeds that with the voice unite ;
Thus to our prayers Thine ears incline,
Such bend the Majesty Divine.

Glory to God both One and Three,
To God Triune all glory be,
Whose word all things to being brought,
Whose word sustains all He hath wrought.

AT THE MATTINS.

"We do not cease to pray for you, and to desire that ye
might be filled with the knowledge of His will, in all
wisdom and spiritual understanding; that ye might walk
worthy of the Lord, unto all pleasing, being fruitful in
every good work, and increasing in the knowledge of
God, strengthened with all might according to His glorious power."—*Colos*. 1.

Rerum Creator omnium,

MAKER of all things, aid our hands,
  In all our works be near,
That our chaste lives may worthier prove
  The name of Christ to bear.

Thou, only mighty, only good,
  Art to Thyself the way,
Thou only, who hast given the law,
  Canst give us to obey.

Perils environ all the road ;
  Our slippery feet control.

That so our steps more stedfastly
  May press on to the goal.

O happy goal, where true repose,
  And peace awaits for ever,
And Thou to Thine dost give to drink
  Of joy, as from a river.

For Thee, good Lord, the heart doth pant,
  For Thee the spirit sighs,
Grant unto those Thy grace hath sav'd
  To win the eternal prize.

AT THE VESPERS.

"Our Saviour, Jesus Christ, gave Himself for us, that He might redeem us from all iniquity, and purify unto Himself a peculiar people, zealous of good works."—*Tit.* ii.

Supreme Motor cordium.

GREAT Mover of all hearts, whose hand
Doth all the secret springs command
    Of human thought and will,
Thou, since the world was made, dost bless
Thy saints with fruits of holiness,
    Their order to fulfil.

Faith, hope, and love, here weave one chain,
But love alone shall then remain,
    When this short day is gone :

THE SEVENTH DAY.

O love, O truth, O endless light,
When shall we see thy Sabbath bright
    With all our labours done ?

We sow 'mid perils here, and tears ;
There the glad hand the harvest bears,
    Which here in grief hath sown.
Great God Triune, the increase give,
And these Thy gifts, by which we live,
    With heavenly glory crown !

HYMNS FOR THE SEASONS.

In Advent.

AT MIDNIGHT.

"Watch ye, and pray always, that ye may be accounted
worthy to stand before the Son of Man."—*Luke* xxi.

Instantis adventum Dei.

Our God approaches from the skies;
  Let us for Him prepare,
With dread prelusive symphonies,
  And deep heart-glowing prayer.

Nor doth the everlasting Son
  Abhor the Virgin's womb:
That we from bondage may be won,
  He bears a servant's doom.

Gentle and meek He comes; arise,
  Sion, behold thy King,
And haste to meet Him, nor despise
  The peace He deigns to bring.

He shall return the Judge e'en now
 On clouds with lightning riven,
And His own body left below
 In triumph bear to Heaven.

Let crimes, the brood of night, depart
 From the approaching morn;
And the old Adam of the heart
 Before the newly-born.

All praise, while endless ages run,
 To Father ever blest,
To Spirit, and eternal Son,
 In flesh made manifest.

AT THE MATTINS.

"Thus speaketh the Lord of Hosts, saying, Behold the man whose name is the Branch; and He shall grow up out of His place, and He shall build the temple of the Lord."—*Zech.* vi.

Jordanis oras prævia.

Lo, the Baptist's herald cry
 Shakes the Jordan;
Let the wakening eye and ear
Welcome the great harbinger.

Earth, and sea, and listening sky,
 Wait their Maker;
And throughout the mighty womb,
Feel the jubilee is come.

Let us cast the way on high,
  For His coming;
Cleanse the heart, and make it meet
For His heaven-descended feet.

Jesu, strength, and solace nigh,
  And salvation !
Without Thee, like withering grass,
Man doth into nothing pass.

Unto us, who pine and die,
  Stretch forth Thy hand ;
Earth shall break her wintry trance
At Thy blissful countenance.

Praise to Him who comes from high,
  Our Deliverer ;
Praise to Father, Spirit, Son,
Never ending, ne'er begun.

AT THE VESPERS.

"At the end it shall speak, and not lie; though it tarry, wait
for it; because it will surely come; it will not tarry."—*Hab. ii.*

Statuta decreto Dei.

DEEP hidden, by divine decree,
In the dark womb of destiny,
The long-delaying day appears,
And shines through clouds of rolling years
  From the descending sky.

By crimes parental helpless made,
Were Adam's offspring wounded laid,
And far within yon gloomy vale
Sat lost, in sorrow's twilight pale,
  And death's o'erhanging shade;

That second death of deathless shame;
The death of everlasting flame;
While on the brow, by Terror writ,
Did dismal Expectation sit
  At Judgment's awful name.

Alas! for downfal so profound
Who shall bring help? whence shall abound
Succour and hope? what hand shall be
Meet for the mighty remedy
  Of that o'erwhelming wound!

O Christ, 'tis Thou, 'tis Thou alone,
Descending from Thy Godhead's throne,
The tarnish'd lineaments once more
To Thy lost image canst restore,
  Thy children to Thy bosom own.

Rain down, ye overhanging skies!
Lost earth looks up with yearning eyes,
And when the Just One shall have come
Into her long-expectant womb,
  From her Salvation shall arise.

To Thee, to clothe Thee with our shame,
Who from Thy Father's bosom came,
The Word Incarnate ; and to Thee,
Father, and Spirit, One and Three,
  Praise everlasting to Thy name.

AT THE COMPLINE.

"Behold the Lord hath proclaimed unto the end of the
world, Say ye to the daughter of Zion, Behold thy Salvation
cometh."—*Isaiah* lxii.

In noctis umbra desides.

AND now, with shades of night opprest,
Our weary limbs are laid at rest,
The faithful soul shall wake and weep,
And unto Thee her vigils keep.

Health of the world, the Father's Word,
By whom our untold prayers are heard,
Desire of nations, hear our sighs,
And raise us from our miseries.

Why do Thy wheels so long delay?
Come Thou, and cast our chains away,
And ope the heavenly doors again,
Which Adam's crime hath closed amain.

Praise to the Son, who cometh down
To make lost man again His own ;
Praise be throughout the days of Heaven
To Father and to Spirit given !

On the Vigil of the Nativity.

AT THE COMPLINE.

Mundi salus qui nasceris.

INFANT, born the world to free,
  Look on us,
That in child-like wisdom we
Put on Thy humility.

Thou that midst the beasts did sleep,
  Helpless babe,
From dark foes that seek Thy sheep,
Sacred Shepherd, save and keep.

Thou who hast Thy Godhead laid
  All aside,
On the breast of mother maid,
To our weakness lend Thine aid.

Thou who op'st the heavenly door,
  Virgin-born,
Three in One whom we adore,
Praise to Thee for evermore.

On the Natibity.

AT THE FIRST VESPERS.

Missum Redemptorem polo.

Let all the earth her King adore
    From furthest pole to pole,
    Where'er the sun doth roll;
Sent forth from the eternal shore
    To visit us forlorn,
    He comes, the Virgin-born.

To save from death those He hath made,
    God, who did all create,
    Puts on a slave's estate;
Born ere the pillar'd world was laid,
    He comes a mortal child,
    To earth and time exil'd.

Our God on a straw pallet lies,
    And infant food is given
    To Him the food of Heaven :
He lies full low that we may rise,
    And the world-wielding hands
    Are bound by swaddling-bands.

He asks returns for such vast love,
  And, though the Judge of all,
  Doth to His cradle call :
Then be all praise to Him above,
  To Father and to Son
  And Spirit ever One.

AT MIDNIGHT.

"I will not rest until the righteousness thereof go forth as brightness, and the salvation thereof as a lamp that burneth."—*Isaiah lxii.*

Jam desinant suspiria.

Away with sorrow's sigh,
Our prayers are heard on high,
And through Heaven's crystal door,
On this our earthly floor
Comes meek-eyed Peace to walk with poor
        mortality.

In dead of night profound
There breaks a seraph sound
Of never-ending morn,—
The Lord of glory born
Within a holy grot on this our sullen ground.

Now with that shepherd crowd,
If it might be allow'd,

We fain would enter there
With awful hastening fear,
And kiss that cradle chaste in reverend wor-
ship bow'd.

O sight of strange surprise,
That fills our gazing eyes,
A manger coldly strew'd,
And swaddling-bands so rude,
A leaning mother poor, and child that help-
less lies.

Art Thou, O wondrous sight,
Of lights the very Light,
Who holdest in Thy hand
The sky and sea and land,
Who than the glorious Heavens art more ex-
ceeding bright?

'Tis so;—faith darts before,
And through the cloud drawn o'er,
She sees the God of all,
Where Angels prostrate fall,
Adoring tremble still, and trembling, still
adore.

No thunders round Thee break,
Yet doth Thy silence speak
From that Thy Teacher's seat
To us around Thy feet,
To shun what flesh desires, what flesh abhors
to seek.

Within us, Babe Divine,
Be born, and make us Thine ;
Within our souls reveal
Thy love and power to heal,
Be born, and make our hearts Thy cradle and
　　　Thy shrine.

AT THE VESPERS.

"In this was manifested the love of God towards us;
because that God sent His only-begotten Son into the
world, that we might live through Him."—1 John iv.

Jesu, Redemptor omnium.

Jesu, born the world to free,
The Incarnate Deity ;
Ere the worlds their march begun,
Equal Thou with God, and One ;
Thou our peace and glory art,
Only hope of mortal heart :
Hear our prayers which to the skies
From the heart's low altar rise,
　　　Holy Son, and unto Thee
　　　Sing we everlastingly.

With a free, spontaneous birth,
Thou didst take a form of earth,
Drawing mortal men to Thee
To partake of Deity.

Us Thy brethren Thou dost call,
Our hand holding, lest we fall,
And our life, with deadly stain,
To its vileness turn again.
  Holy Spirit, unto Thee
  Sing we everlastingly.

This is the glad holiday,
Which in memory holds the ray,
When from out His shining bed
The true Sun did lift His head,—
And the earth and distant pole
And where ocean's waters roll,—
Each in holy ardor vies
Breaking forth in jubilees,
  Holy Father, unto Thee
  Singing everlastingly.

Nor shall we, for whom undone
Comes the everlasting Son,
Let in thankless silence stay
This our first-born holiday !
Praise Him, creatures here below ;
Him, where'er His blessings flow ;
Him, earth, sea, and heavenly host ;
Father, Son, and Holy Ghost :
  Dreadful name of Godhead, Thee
  Sing we everlastingly.

St. Stephen's Day.

AT MIDNIGHT.

"Be thou faithful unto death, and I will give thee a crown of life."—Rev. ii.

O, qui tuo, dux Martyrum.

Rightful Prince of martyrs thou,
Bind thy crown about thy brow;
Fairer far than fading wreath,
Weave we this thy crown of death.

Like a gem each rugged stone,
Sparkling with thy life-blood, shone;
Nor could stars more brightly shine,
Studded round thy head divine.

From thy forehead's gushing streams
Dart a thousand blending beams,
Till thy glowing countenance
Lightens to an Angel's glance.

Thou the first-slain victim free
To Him, the Victim slain for thee:
Thou the first thy Lord to own,
Sharer of His thorny crown.

First to tread the pointed road
Through the deep Red sea of blood :—
Prince of martyrs, thee behind
What a countless army wind !

Thou of Virgin-mother born,
In this wintry world forlorn ;
   Jesu, Lord, all praise to Thee.
All glory be to Father, Son,
And Holy Spirit, Three in One,
   Unto all eternity.

AT THE MATTINS.

"Behold my witness is in Heaven, and my record is
on high."—Job xvi.

Quid obstinata pectora.

Why, stern of heart, and dull of ear,
  The heaven-born truth defy ?
When full of Heaven he bids you hear,
  Why doom the saint to die ?

Behold him, where each murderous hand
  Upheaves the deadly stone ;
And Saul hath arm'd his savage band
  Around yon guiltless one.

How fruitless all ! for lo, on high
    Heaven's starry court expands,
And far beyond the opening sky
    Th' enthronèd Saviour stands.

Thou fail'st not, Lord, Thy liegeman true,
    Amidst the struggle hard,
Thou art his might, his umpire Thou,
    And Thou his great reward.

Nor recks he aught the 'whelming shower,
    Full fix'd on Heaven and Thee :
Where Thou art Judge, and Thine the power,
    To die is victory.

From Thy full fount his raptur'd thought
    Drinks in Thy living fires ;
And from his mortal coil up-caught,
    He joins Thine Angel quires.

Oh Thou, of Virgin-mother born,
    Jesu, all praise to Thee :
All glory be to Father, Son,
And Holy Spirit, Three in One,
    To all eternity.

AT THE VESPERS.

"I say unto you, Love your enemies, bless them that curse
you, do good to them that hate you, and pray for them that
despitefully use you and persecute you, that ye may be the children of your Father which is in Heaven."—*St. Matt.* v.

Miris probat sese modis.

HOLY Love towards her foes
In mysterious channels flows ;
Bow'd to soothe, or steel'd to blame,
Holy Love is still the same.

Pleader for himself he stood :—
Now he falls, his eloquent blood
From the ground for mercy cries,
Pleading for his enemies.

God from Heaven His martyr heard,—
Heard, and bless'd his dying word :
Saul, the murderer, standing by,—
Saul was granted to that cry.

Thus he bow'd his drooping head,
Thus his joyous spirit fled :
" Jesu, Lord," his offering free,—
" Take the life I owe to Thee."

Death, kind angel, watching nigh,
Sweetly clos'd his tranquil eye;
Whilst the freed spirit wing'd her flight,
From beam to beam, to endless light.

Thou that dealtst thy plenteous store
Daily to the sick and poor,
Now art come, a welcome guest,
To thy Father's table blest.

In thy bridal crown display'd,
In the wedding-robe array'd
Of thy purple life-blood wove,
For the Slain One's feast of love.

Thou of Virgin-mother born,
In this wintry world forlorn,
  Jesu, Lord, all praise to Thee.
All glory be to Father, Son,
And Holy Spirit, Three in One,
  Unto all eternity.

St. John the Evangelist's Day.

AT MIDNIGHT.

"The Lord Himself is the portion of mine inheritance and of
my cup: Thou maintainest my lot."—*Psalm xvi.*

Tu quem præ reliquis Christus amaverat.

THOU, whom before the rest,
The love of Jesus bless'd ;
Thou darling of the Incarnate Deity,
Sharer of all His woes,
Friend of His dying throes,
Eye-witness of His awful sovereignty.

Too-favour'd thou of Heaven,
Oh thou, to whom 'twas given
To touch with mortal hand th' immortal Lord ;
With mortal ear and eye
To hear and see him nigh,
And hold high converse with th' eternal Word.

How mighty was the boon,
When oft to thee alone
Thy Lord in love His secret soul display'd,—
When on His mountain-throne
To thee reveal'd He shone,
Full God, full man in Deity array'd.

Thou, as on Jesus' breast
All peaceful thou dost rest,
Drink'st of the living streams of Deity.
Whilst on thy cleansèd sense
With silent influence
More closely steals His dread Divinity.

Oh cup too full, too high,
For poor mortality !
Thy raptur'd spirit fled its laggard clay.
Say,—when in calm repose
Thy trancèd eyelids close,
To what bright dreams of Heaven they waken,
say.

Oh access dread ! oh bliss
Of mutual love ! ere this
To every soul in every age unknown !
When such the altar-fire,
That lights thy pure desire,
What countless rays it scatters from its
throne !

Hence art thou ever prov'd
Loving, and ever lov'd ;
Hence thy bright brow, and virgin modesty ;
Hence all that heavenly beam,
That Angels might beseem,
Pour'd round thy head, a circling galaxy.

Hence o'er and o'er again
Thy thrice-repeated strain,
Whate'er thou say'st, "" 'tis love, 'tis love

Scarce doth the struggling soul
    Her ecstasy control,
But bursts her bonds, and vents her holy fires.

Glory on high to Thee,
    Holy, eternal Three,
Father and Son and Holy Spirit blest !
    Lo, this the stedfast law,
    The stedfast faith we draw,
From out Thy sacred fount by Heaven's own
        hand express'd.

AT THE MATTINS.

"And I saw another angel fly in the midst of Heaven, having the everlasting gospel to preach unto them that dwell on the earth, and to every nation, and kindred, and tongue, and people, saying with a loud voice, Fear God, and give glory to Him."—Rev. xiv.

Quem nox et tenebræ, densaque nubila.

OH, may my God, whom shade, and night,
        And folded cloud
In viewless brightness rob'd, enshroud,
In mercy veil His fearful light,
Nor whelm His servant's trembling sight !

Belov'd of God, to thee 'twas given
        Unscath'd to see
The blaze of present Deity ;
To see the veil in sunder riven,
And search the inmost court of Heaven.

Borne as on eagle-wings away
    Through ether far,
Thy soul outstrips the utmost star,
Nor Heaven's own lightning's fiery ray
Thy spirit from its God can stay.

Lo! there 'tis thine still on to move
    Thy nearer ken,
Where ear, and eye, and soul of men
Turn in mute awe, and shrink to prove
The mysteries of redeeming love.

For of that love how vast the sum!
    That Deity
Forgetful of itself should be,
And down to earth an exile come,
To lead these wandering exiles home.

'Tis thine Heaven's deepest rites to tell
    To seers divining;
Thou op'st the light in darkness shining:
Thou searchest life's o'erflowing well,
And Heaven-born light's primæval cell.

All praise to God on high we sing,
    To Father, Son,
And Holy Spirit, Three in One.
Lo! this the stedfast creed we bring
Drawn from high Heaven's eternal spring.

AT THE VESPERS.

"Jesus answered and said, Are ye able to drink of the cup
that I shall drink of? They say unto Him, We are able. And
He saith unto them, Ye shall indeed drink of My cup."—
St. Matt. xx.

Sit qui rite canat te modo virginem.

OH, for a saint like thee,
To sing thy virgin purity!
Sing thee Apostle, and unroll
Thy Heaven-taught truth's far-beaming
  scroll,
Or link thee with the seers divine.—
To sing thee martyr-saint, be mine.

For thou, for thou didst view
That death of deaths, companion true!
In spirit with thy Lord wert torn
By facking cross, and piercing thorn;
The only converse left to thee,
Th' high converse of that agony.

There, as in death He hung,
His mantle soft on thee He flung
Of filial love, and nam'd thee son,
When now that earthly tie was done;
To thy tried faith, and spotless years
Consign'd His Virgin-mother's tears.

Could holier charge be given?
True mother of the Lord of Heaven,
Hail'd mother by Himself to thee,
And thou that mother's son as He!
Call'd, as th' Immortal deign'd to die
That loss of losses to supply!

And when His voice was fled,
His lingering look on thee He shed;
Thee, His belov'd disciple, taught
His dying eye's mysterious thought.
When from that blood-stain'd Mercy-
        throne
To all the world His glory shone.

Friend of thy Lord, be mine
My faltering step to match with thine;
To follow onward to the goal
Where love led on thy dauntless soul;
Be mine, as thine, the blessing high,
With Christ to live, with Christ to die.

Glory to Father, Son,
And Spirit, Eternal Three in One.
Lo! this the stedfast creed we bring
Drawn from high Heaven's eternal spring.

The Innocents' Day.

AT MIDNIGHT.

"Suffer little children to come unto Me; for of such is
the kingdom of Heaven."—*Matt. xix.*

Salvete flores martyrum.

LITTLE flowers of martyrdom,
  Whom the ruthless sword hath torn,
  On the threshold of the morn,
  Rosebuds by the whirlwind shorn!

All regardless of their doom,
  'Neath the altar where they lay,
  With their palm and chaplets gay,
  Little simple ones they play.

Tyrant, what avails their tomb?
  He shall 'scape the bloody blade,
  Which hath many childless made,
  Infant born of mother-maid.

Thus the type of Him to come,
  Restorer of lost Israel,
  Moses 'scaped the tyrant fell,
  Guarded by the Invisible.

Jesu, born of Virgin's womb,
    Father, Spirit, One and Three,
    Sing we glory unto Thee,
    Sing we everlastingly.

AT MIDNIGHT.

"They serve God day and night in His temple: they shall
hunger no more, neither thirst any more. The Lamb which
is in the midst of the throne shall lead them unto living
fountains of waters."—*Rev.* vii.

Molles in agnos ceu lupus.

As the wolf in fierceness sore
    Falls on lambs o'er fold and fence,
    Thus the tyrant lost to sense
    Falls on harmless innocents.

And the cradles flow with gore—
    God of gods shall he withstand?
    One he seeks in murder'd band,
    One escapes his murderous hand.

Mourning mothers, weep no more!
    Weep no more your pledges torn,
    Little troop in endless morn
    They attend the Virgin-born.

Virgin-born whom we adore,
    Father, Spirit, One and Three,
    Sing we glory unto Thee,
    Sing we everlastingly.

On the Circumcision.

AT THE FIRST VESPERS.

" What the law could not do, in that it was weak through the flesh, God sending His own Son in the likeness of sinful flesh, and for sin, condemned sin in the flesh; that the righteousness of the law might be fulfilled in us, who walk not after the flesh, but after the spirit."—*Rom.* viii.

Debilis cessent elementa legis.

YE legal elements,
Your clouds of fear remove,
That Christ may come forth to dispense
The eternal law of love.

True sun without a cloud,
O'er heavenly heights He trod ;
Now veil'd beneath a mortal shroud,
The image of our God.

Already stain'd with blood,
The signs of sin He feels,
That precious drop which now ha'b flow'd
For death the victim seals.

This day hath given the Name
To which the world shall bow,
And Thou beginnest with that claim
A Saviour's part to show.

All praise to God all good,
The Father thron'd on high,
The Son who bought us with His blood,
The Spirit ever nigh.

AT MIDNIGHT.

"The Word was made flesh, and dwelt among us, full of grace and truth; and of His fulness have all we received, and grace for grace. For the law was given by Moses, but grace and truth came by Jesus Christ."—John I.

Felix dies, quam proprio.

O HAPPY day, when this our state
With Jesus' blood was consecrate!
O happy day, when first the Lord began
To bare the arm which rescued ruin'd man.

Scarce born in this our solitude
The little infant pours His blood;
To be the earnest of His endless love,
The prelibation of His death to prove.

Entering the world, His Father's will
Instant He hastens to fulfil;
And is beforehand with the day of death,
Mark'd as the victim ere He yields His breath.

In very pity for our thrall,
He thus becomes the criminal;
Made 'neath the law, He hastes its yoke to bear,
That from that yoke He may His people spare.

The law is slain by that same sword
By which it dares to smite the Lord;
A holier law begins which shall prevail,
The holier law of love which cannot fail.

Thee of a Virgin-mother born,
In whom is centred endless morn,
We praise Thee, bless Thee, worship and adore,
With Father, and with Spirit, evermore.

AT THE MATTINS.

"Our Saviour, Jesus Christ, gave Himself for us, that He might redeem us from all iniquity, and purify unto Himself a peculiar people zealous of good works."—*Titus* ii.

Noxium Christus simul introivit.

When Christ enter'd the world, and it lay still,
"Father," He said, "I come to do Thy will,
"I come prepared, let Justice take her fill,
    "'Tis written in Thy book, and I arise.

"Offering Thou would'st not, then said I,
        I come,
"A body Thou preparest Me; from the womb
"A dying Lamb, I take the sinner's doom,
    "And am Myself the only sacr.fice."

He spake, and did Himself to God afford
To bear the stern wounds of the legal sword,
Fulfilling all the law,—the living Word,
   He pays alone the forfeit penalties.

Ah, vain the task to stop sin's mantling shoot,
Man from the heart must weed the bitter root,
While the new law engrafted puts forth fruit,
   And drinks the blessing of the pitying skies.

Not unto us, but Thee, Father of Heaven,
Not unto us, but Thee, the Son, be given,
Not unto us, but Thee, from morn till even,
   Good Spirit, unto Thee our hymns arise.

AT THE SECOND VESPERS.

Victis sibi cognomina.

"Whatsoever ye do in word or deed, do all in the name
of the Lord Jesus, giving thanks to God and the Father
by Him."—Coloss. iii.

LET earthly tyrants title claim
   From each conquer'd nation,
Thou, Lord, shalt take a worthier name
   Which hath wrought salvation;
The name which wretched men may plead
The Resurrection of the dead,
   And pledge of life that knows no dying.

The name which He hath bought with blood,
  And with keenest sadness :
Shall we then forfeit all our good
  In short-sighted madness ?
The highest boon we can receive
Is for that sacred name to grieve
  Which takes from death the sting of anguish.

Jesu, hear Thou our sorrow's plaint,
  Thou art all our glory ;
And known to Thee is every want
  Ere we come before Thee.
To Thee, the Son, our voice we raise,
Father and Spirit, Thee we praise,
  All love to Thee, all adoration.

On the Epiphany.

AT THE FIRST VESPERS.

"There shall be a root of Jesse, and He that shall
rise to reign over the Gentiles; in Him shall the Gentiles trust."—Rom. xv.

Quæ stella sole pulchrior.

WHAT is that which shines afar,
Fairer than the sun at morn?
'Tis a glorious star,
Which a rising King doth harbinger,
And marks a cradle low where God on earth
is born.
Faithful spake ye, seers of old,
From Jacob doth a Star arise,
The East is stirrèd to behold.
A little star keeps watch without,
'Tis let down from the skies;
But a nobler Star within
Doth its march begin,
Which, on their distant rout,
To Him with gentle power doth lead the Wise.
The toil and perils what are they?
Faithful love knows no delay:
Kindred, and home, and country hold not them;

'Tis God that calls, and they obey.
Star of Bethlehem,
Star of Grace, that lead'st the way,
Let not the mists of our dark soul
Obstruct Thy heavenly light, and guiding soft
control.
Father, Light of lights, to Thee,
To Holy Spirit, and to Son,
In whom Thou to the world hast shone,
Everlasting glory be !

AT THE MATTINS.

"God hath saved us, and called us with an holy calling, not according to our works, but according to His own purpose and grace, which was given us in Christ Jesus before the world began, but is now made manifest by the appearing of our Lord Jesus Christ."—2 Tim. i.

Linquunt tecta Magi principis urbis.

From princely walls in Eastern pomp array'd,
They seek the distant Bethlehem's lowly
shade ;
Faith leads the way, and gathers light, and
now
Leans upon hope, which strengthens as
they go.

What gladness crown'd their steps as now
to view
The Heavenly Messenger appeared anew ;

And o'er the roof the star descending mild
Shewed in a mother's arms the Holy Child!

But yet no ivory here, no glowing gold,
No purple royalties the Babe enfold;
His palace-hall—a stable's solitude,
His regal throne—a manger dark and rude!

Others let Kingly pomp and power adorn,
His is a better Kingship; on this morn
He, on His poor straw pallet meanly laid,
Hath hearts of men with viewless sceptre
        sway'd.

Lo, at His humble cradle, on bent knee,
They in the Child adore the Deity!
And to that Child us of that Gentile seed,
And to that humble cradle Faith shall lead.

Love is the gold, meet offering for a King,
Myrrh to the Son of Man shall abstinence
        bring;
And prayers shall be the ascending frank-
        incense
Which owns our God in veil'd Omnipotence.

Glory to God the Father, Fount of Light,
To Him, who shone upon the Gentiles' night,
And unto Him, well-spring of Charity,
All equal in mysterious Unity!

AT THE VESPERS.

Huc vos, o miseri, surda relinquite.

Poor wanderers, who make your prayer
  To gods form'd by your hands,
That speak and hear not—see ye where
  A glorious city stands,
And opes to you her walls and golden rest;
Those glorious walls within God is Himself
    the guest.

E'en now your chiefs they lead the way,
  The volume is displayed,
From prophecy breaks forth the ray :—
  They sat beneath death's shade,
But wake, and see afar a wondrous light,
Which from those walls breaks forth upon the
    rear of night.

Long have they been asunder thrown,
  Like sunshine and the shade;
But now—the wall is broke and gone,
  And they are equal made;
Oh Thou, whose counsels in dark waters
    dwell,
And footsteps are in deeps by man un-
    traceable

Judah, who on her mountain throne
　　Had built on high her nest,
Hath from her lofty seat come down
　　To welcome her new Guest.
And see the Alien's glory late made wise,
To live by her decay, from her abasement rise.

Drooping and dropping as she hung
　　Over her stock o'erthrown,
She sees new shoots around her sprung,
　　And branches not her own!
Ah me, take heed, thou faith-engrafted shoot,
Lest thou be sever'd from the Life-supporting
　　　　Root!

Glory to Thee, the Living Three,
　　The Everlasting Son,
And Thee, who gavest us to be
　　Made in that Body one,
And Spirit, spreading life through every limb,
Oh! graft again the lost—the grafted keep in
　　　　Him.

Until the Octabe of the Epiphany.

AT MIDNIGHT.

"Men of stature shall come over unto thee, and they shall
be thine, they shall come after thee, they shall fall down unto
thee; they shall make supplication unto thee, saying, Surely
God is in thee; and there is none else, there is no God."—
Isaiah xlv.

Quâ lapsu tacito stella loquacibus.

THE star before doth stilly glide
   With gently-speaking rays,
The seers pursue the wondrous guide
   With earnest feet and gaze;
And now the heaven-led wanderers come
To towering Salem's mountain home,
   And there have lost the friendly star,
As in his darkling mid career
The star deserts the mariner
   On nightly seas afar.

They little deem of envious arts,
   No princely wrath they fear,
But for their King, with guileless hearts,
   They seek both far and near;

Faith ne'er shall simple hearts deceive,
For though the heavenly Star may leave,
  From Holy Writ breaks forth the light;
The strangers to the King are brought,
By His own people set at nought,
  And witness the dread sight.

And we with them would praise our King
The Father, Son, and Spirit sing,
  The Spirit who doth from both proceed;
The herald star may guide the feet,
But Thou alone, blest Paraclete,
  Can the dark spirit lead.

On the Octave of the Epiphany.

AT THE FIRST VESPERS.

"Jerusalem shall be holy, and there shall no stranger pass through her any more; and it shall come to pass in that day that the mountains shall drop down new wine, and the hills shall flow with milk, and all the rivers of Jordan shall overflow with waters, and a fountain shall come forth of the house of the Lord, and shall water the valley of thorns."—*Joel* iii.

Clamantis, ecce, vox sonans.

JUDÆA's desert heard a sound
   Of one that cried aloud,
They flocked the holy John around
   With sin and sadness bowed.

Lo, 'mid that guilty company
   A sinless Lamb drew near,
His blood alone that crowd can free
   From guilt and shame and fear.

Before the sun a taper dim,
   John stands, and meekly pleads,
Nor pours the hallowing wave; of Him
   The Baptist washing needs.

But to obey his God 'tis meet,
   Though He Himself depress,
Prepar'd all fulness to complete,
   Perfect in righteousness.

Confessor, and great Harbinger,
　Thou Baptist of the wave,
The Baptist He of living fire
　The secret soul to lave !

To Him who wash'd us with His blood,
　As hath been heretofore,
To Father, and to Spirit good,
　Be glory evermore.

AT MIDNIGHT.

"These waters issue out toward the East; they shall be healed, and every thing shall live whither the river cometh; because their waters issued out of the sanctuary."—*Ezek.* xlvii.

Non abluunt lymphæ Deum.

It is not that the wave can wash our God,
　But that our God doth wash the limpid wave;
Touch'd by His flesh, as by a healing rod,
　Water hath learn'd new virtue, strong to
　　save.

The fountain long foretold is open free,
　From guilty spot to wash the heart unseen ;
O miracle of wondrous potency,
　The flesh is wash'd—the sin-stain'd soul is
　　clean !

'Tis thus, immersed within the sacred flood,
　The royal purple of the King of Woe
Hath　turn'd　the　natural　wave　to　mystic
　　　blood,
　　Making robes wash'd therein all white as
　　　snow.

The Holy Spirit on a virgin came,
　　Thence God to　us　is　born　in　wondrous
　　　love ;
Upon the hallowed water came the same,
　　And we therein are born to God above.

To Thee, who washest the lost world with
　　　blood,
　All glory be as hath been heretofore ;
With Father, and with Spirit, only good,
　　As hath been, is, and shall be evermore.

AT THE MATTINS.

"Then will I sprinkle clean water upon you, and ye shall be
clean.　A new heart also will I give you, and a new spirit will
I put within you; and I will take away the stony heart out o f
your flesh, and I will give you an heart of flesh."—*Ezek.* xxxvi.

Emergit undis, et Deo.

He rises from the wave, and now
To God on high, God-Man below,
He prays—that prayer is said ;

The Courts of Heaven afar extending,
And Holy Ghost is seen descending
  Upon that sacred Head,

E'en like a hovering dove : the Word
Of God, the Father, now is heard—
  "This is My Son belov'd!"
Around, afar, above, and under,
Like to mysterious, holiest thunder,
  The deepening echoes mov'd.

Lo, wash'd within that hallowing tide,
By Jesus' body sanctified,
  A people newly born !
And to their prayers the opening heaven,
To them to be God's sons is given,
  And walk in endless morn !

Emblem of unstain'd purity,
And sacred, mild simplicity,
  Descends the mystic Dove ;
And on their hearts divinely reigning,
Protecting, cherishing, sustaining,
  Prepares for God above.

We have been wash'd within the fountain
Flowing from out Thy sacred mountain !
  For aye with us remain ;—
O Saviour, who hast shed Thy blood
To wash our souls and make us good,
  Keep us from sinful stain.

And we, through all our earthly days,
Would sing in Thee our Maker's praise,
   For Thou hast made us meet;
Let creatures all, of earth and sky,
The Son and Father glorify,
   And Holy Paraclete.

On the Sundays from the Octave of the Epiphany.

AT THE FIRST VESPERS.

"With a voice of singing declare ye, tell this, utter it even to the end of the earth; say ye, The Lord hath redeemed His servant Jacob."—*Isaiah* xlviii.

Verbum quod ante sæcula.

WORD of Life, the eternal Son,
Ere the march of time begun,
Now as man He deigns to come,
Offspring of the Virgin's womb,
From our limbs to burst in twain
Fallen Adam's fatal chain;
All we lost in Thee returns,
And our hope reviving burns.

Thou dost bear the ills e'en now
Such as guilt doth undergo;
Cries that from Thy cradle rose
Presage now Thy dying woes.
Thou art poor, that we may be
Rich in Thy deep poverty.
Thou dost weep, and by Thy woe
Washest all things here below.

Thou art wrapp'd in garments mean,
Lying in a cave unclean:
Man is proud; yet Deity
In so mean a hut doth lie.
Jesu, by the Father sent
To bear our due punishment,
Leave us not to be undone
By such deep abasement won.

Endless praise to Thee be paid,
Jesu, born of mother maid;
Thee, with Father evermore,
And with Spirit we adore.

AT MIDNIGHT.

"O the hope of Israel, the Saviour thereof in time of trouble, why shouldest Thou be as a stranger in the land, and as a wayfaring man that turneth aside to tarry for a night? Why shouldest Thou be as a man astonied, as a mighty man that cannot save?"—*Jerem.* xiv.

Fac, Christe, nostri gratiâ.

Christ, to aid our fallen nature,
    Thou didst bear bereavements stern,
Grant we such with spirits holy,
    And with grateful hymns return;
Though eternal born, yet Thou would'st learn to die,
        to die,
And didst put on the shape of frail humanity.

Soon as born, a helpless infant,
  Thou didst suffer winter's cold ;
For a couch of costly purple,
  Hay-bands rude Thy form enfold :
Pitying us, to need our pity Thou dost seem,
And yieldest to the law, the Lawgiver supreme.

The blood its stern behest requires
  From Thy deepest heart doth come ;
The sword that slays the harmless infants,
  To Thy breast it pierces home ;—
Lo, to Pharos now, an exile poor, He flies,
The true God mix'd with foul and lying deities.

But with hosts of highest Heaven,
  Hence Thy ransom'd heritage
Shall, with lowest adoration,
  Worship Thee from age to age ;
Father eternal, and Thee, eternal Son,
And Thee, eternal Spirit, Three in One.

———

AT THE MATTINS.

"Till we all come in the unity of the faith, and of the knowledge of the Son of God, unto a perfect man, unto the measure of the stature of the fulness of Christ: that we henceforth be no more children, tossed to and fro, and carried about with every wind of doctrine."—*Ephes.* iv.

Divine, crescebas, puer.

AND Thou art growing up, O Child divine!
  While on Thy life a daily dying lies ;
All things that open on this life of Thine
  Are preludes to Thy dying agonies.

God, born of God, Himself He fain would hide
With a mean sire the scorn of human pride;
And He who moulded heaven's o'erarching
    dome
In a poor earthly cottage makes His home.

  Hands, that sustain the pillars of heaven's
    roof,
    Handle the ignoble craft of feeble man;
  The Framer of the stars, that speed aloof,
    Himself becomes a low-housed artizan.
Lo, He who hath the world beneath His feet,
He at whose dread behest Archangels fleet,
And far and wide His Kingly mandates bear,
Is subject to an humble carpenter.

Jesu, the Maiden-born, to Thee we sing—
Father, Son, Spirit; Maker, Lord, and King;—
Glory to Thee, when earth and heaven have
    gone,
And everlasting Time his course hath run.

AT THE VESPERS.

"The Word whom God sent unto the children of Israel, preaching peace by Jesus Christ, He is Lord of all."—*Acts x.*

Christus tenebris obsitam.

AND now Heaven's growing light is manifest
Through Judah's land, which in the darkness
    lies;
    But they have steel'd their breast,
    And closed their earth-bound eyes.

Now signs of present Godhead teem around,
The dead are rais'd, feet to the lame are given,
   The dumb a tongue hath found,
   The blind man sees the heaven.

But Israel hath become blind, deaf, and dead;
He is their Sun; but they, like birds of night,
   To unclean haunts have fled,
   And will not brook the light.

But we would turn to Thee, and court the ray;
Thou art the eternal Father's Charity;
   And never-setting day
   For ever dwells in Thee.

Let not the night creep o'er us, Light divine;
Let not the night creep o'er our hearts below;
   With Thy truth may they shine,
   With Thy love burn and glow.

To Thee, with Father and with Spirit blest,
Jesu, to Thee, born of a Maiden pure,
   Be highest praise addrest,
   And evermore endure.

On the Seventh Day before Septuagesima.

AT THE VESPERS.

"The children of Israel shall keep the sabbath, to observe the sabbath throughout their generations, for a perpetual covenant. It is a sign between Me and the children of Israel for ever: for in six days the Lord made heaven and earth, and on the seventh day He rested."—*Exodus* xxxi.

Te læta, mundi Conditor.

THOU, Lord, in endless rest,
   Dost Thy sure Sabbath keep,
Where angels ever blest,
   Do sing and never sleep;
To us, from virtue fallen, toils belong,
For how can exiles sad sing their lost country's
     song?

But Thou art pledged to spare
   On tears of penitence;
Grant us to mourn with stedfast care
   The sins that keep us thence,
That faith and hope may temper healthful woes,
Until we be restored to Thy secure repose.

Thee, Lord, where in Thy rest,
    Thou dost Thy Sabbath keep,
May angels, ever blest,
    Sing Thee, and never sleep—
Sing Father, Son, and Holy Spirit divine,
And we, though exiles sad, our feebler strain
        combine.

On the Sundays from Septuagesima till Lent.

AT MIDNIGHT.

" As the heavens are higher than the earth, so are My ways higher than your ways; for as the rain cometh down and the snow from heaven, and watereth the earth, that it may give seed to the sower and bread to the eater, so shall My word be that goeth forth out of My mouth."—*Isaiah* lv.

Rebus creatis nil egens.

Thou of the things created nothing needing,
  Wert hid in Thine essential blessedness,
But from Thine own mysterious shrine pro-
    ceeding,
    Didst speak the word which doth with being
      bless ;
      And things that were not to Thy hand
Before Thee instant all in duteous order stand,
  And to the great Creator lift the song,
    With multitudinous tongue ;
  And round Thy throne the buoyant welkin
    hung,
So beauteous the great world from Thine own
    bosom sprung.

But Thou, e'en then, a nobler work, O Lord,
  Of holiness and beauty undefil'd,
Wert meditating, which the Eternal Word
  Shall of His own unfading graces build;
    Yea, He Himself shall forth proceed,
And therein far and wide scatter the living seed.
  He that new world, when time's career is
    done,
    Shall place beside His throne;
  And to His gracious Father shall present,
E'en as a spotless bride in glorious ornament.

Thou both these worlds dost lighten, Holy Son,
And Thou both worlds dost hallow, Spirit
    Divine,
Thou, Father, both dost keep,—the Three in
    One,
Father, and Son, and Spirit,—all praise be
    Thine.

AT THE MATTINS.

"Thou art worthy, O Lord, to receive glory and honour and
power: for Thou hast created all things, and for Thy pleasure
they are and were created."—*Rev.* iv.

Qui nos creas solus, Pater.

THOU, Lord, alone dost us create,
But not alone dost renovate,
  But Thy sure promise give,
And stretchest forth Thine aiding hand,
Requiring that at Thy command
  We seize Thy hand and live.

Thy mercy meets the penitent ;
To loiterers are Thy warnings sent,
  To break their growing chains ;
And, like Thine awful Self, within
There *something* is denouncing sin,
  And working silent pains.

Then health, with bitter pangs retrieved,
Dread admonition hath achieved
  A stricter watch to keep :
O love, educing good from ill,
O wisdom strange, inscrutable,
  Of Him that walks the deep.

Thy footsteps in dark waters move,
And like the sky is Thy vast love,
  Thy wrath is fearful known,
As when the unheeding world was drown'd,
And 'mid the o'erwhelming seas profound,
  Was Noah saved alone.

Preacher of Righteousness, to plant
The new life-giving covenant,
  On seas without a shore,
He went o'er the baptismal flood,—
The world's new sire, alone found good,
  Christ's figure true He bore.

To Him who through all time and space
Lifts on His saints His beaming face,
  Things heavenly, things below.
To Father, Son, and Sp'rit Divine,
Who in their saints united shine,
  The earth and heaven shall bow.

AT THE VESPERS.

"These all died in faith, not having received the promises, but having seen them afar off, and were persuaded of them, and embraced them, and confessed that they were strangers and pilgrims upon the earth."—*Heb.* xi.

Vos ante Christi tempora.

Ye patriarchal saints and sires,
  And Christ's prophetic seers,
Ye of just men the solemn choirs,
Studding the heavens with your dim fires,
  Ere yet the dawn appears !

And who can paint Faith's earnest guise,
  Which on the unopened door
Bent eager its inquiring eyes ?
And who can speak Hope's heart-sick sighs
  Which, panting, looked before ?

Strangers were ye, and sojourners,
  Your sylvan homes among ;
The world to you truth's figure bears ;
And 'neath the word's dead characters
  Ye hear the Spirit's tongue.

Thus promised good in time's dark womb
  Did ye divinely weigh :
Grant we o'er this ethereal dome
May ever turn to our true home,
  And look before as they.

To God the Father let us sing,
  To praise Him is most meet;
To God the Son we touch the string,
To God the Spirit we worship bring,
  To praise Him is most sweet.

In the Season of Lent.

AT MIDNIGHT.

"Cast away from you all your transgressions; and make
you a new heart, and a new spirit. For I have no pleasure
in the death of him that dieth, saith the Lord God: where-
fore turn yourselves, and live ye."—*Ezek.* xviii.

Quod lex adumbravit vetus.

IT is the holy fast,
Which Christ hath sanctified,
Shadow'd of ages past
For them who to the world have died.

Let there be holy guard
O'er word, and food, and sleep,
That in her widow'd ward,
The soul her strictest watch may keep.

That so she best within
Her rebel lusts may quell,
Lest the dark foe, unseen,
Steal in and seize the citadel.

Let us bow down and weep,
Ere yet it be too late,
His path with tears to steep
Before the Judge be at the gate.

Tremendous Judge, e'en now
Our crimes like mountains rise,
But yet a Father Thou,
And mightier are Thy clemencies.

Frail as the potter's clay,
But yet Thy work are we:
O leave us not a prey
For whom Christ paid the penalty.

Heal us from all our sin,
Restore us to our place,
With contrite hearts to win
Thine all-abounding pitying grace.

This boon on us confer,
Our Father and our Lord,
And Thou, sole Comforter,
Of godly woe the fruits afford.

AT THE MATTINS.

"Cry aloud, spare not, lift up thy voice like a trumpet,
and shew My people their transgressions, and the house
of Jacob their sins."—Isaiah lviii.

Solemne nos jejunii.

AND now the season grave and deep
Unto the solemn temple calls,
The priest laments, and sounds that weep,
With prayers for mercy fill the walls.

But vainly penitential cries
To our offended God would rise,
Unless the sounds that speak of sin
But echo the deep voice that doth lament within.

Nought ashes on the forehead spread,
Nor garments profit rent and torn ;
But hearts awak'ning from the dead,
And torn and rent by sighs that mourn,
And tears upon the pallid cheek,
Which the deep labouring spirit speak,
May turn away His hand e'en now,
When He hath ta'en His shafts and bent the
          deadly bow.

Thou Judge of justice, holy God,
O turn a little while away,
Turn aside Thine avenging rod,
And give us time and hearts to pray.
O Three in One, bless'd God above,
O One in Three, great God of love,
Bless and make fruitful this our fast,
Lest that repentance need when it hath gone
          and past.

AT THE VESPERS.

"If the wicked walk in the statutes of life, without committing iniquity, he shall surely live, he shall not die. None of the sins that he hath committed shall be mentioned unto him."—*Ezek.* xxxiii.

Audi, benigne Conditor.

Merciful Maker, hear our call,
On idle winds O let not all
  Our prayers and tears be spent
    In sacred Lent.

Thou who dost know each hidden part,
And with Thy sunbeam search the heart,
  We unto Thee return,
    O, do not spurn.

Much have we sinnèd, we confess,
Spare us ! O, for our helplessness,
  Upon us pity take,
    For Thy Name's sake.

May the stern rein of abstinence
So bring the body down, that thence
  The soul may watch and pray
    Her stains away.

Grant, One in Three, blest Trinity,
Grant, Three in One, blest Unity,
  Our Lent may blessèd prove
    In fruits of love.

AT THE COMPLINE.

"Be sober, be vigilant; because your adversary, the devil,
as a roaring lion, walketh about, seeking whom He may
devour; whom resist stedfast in the faith."—1 *Peter* v.

O splendor æterni Patris.

O CHRIST, blest effluence Divine,
True Day, true Light, of lights the Light
    That on the heart doth shine,
    Scattering the spirit's night.

Lo, the tired sun hath gone to rest,
As night's alternate brow arose,
    Thou, who the day hast blest,
    Bless us in our repose.

That, though our eyes to slumber yield,
The yearning soul may be above;
    We hide us 'neath Thy shield,
    We hang upon Thy love.

That, though this outward weary gloom
Weigh us, the soul may find a wing,
    And to its holy home
    For ever soar and sing.

Hear us, our only Help and Health,
Whom Thou hast purchased to be good,
   Paying the countless wealth
   Of Thine own holy blood.

To God the Father, God the Son,
And God the Spirit, glory be,
   Co-equal Three in One,
   To all eternity.

On the First Friday in Lent.

AT THE VESPERS.

"I will pour upon the house of David, and upon the inhabitants of Jerusalem, the spirit of grace and of supplications; and they shall look upon Me whom they have pierced."—Zech. xii.

Prome rocem, mens, canoram.

Draw out, sad heart, thy melody,
    And tell with plaintive cry
The sorrows of the Crucified,
    The wounds of Him that died,
Him, who a willing victim came
    To die a spotless Lamb.

By that unpitying fury kill'd,
    Our ransom He fulfill'd;
We drink health from His bitter cup,
    His Cross doth lift us up,
His stripes for us a balm have found,
    'Tis He our wounds hath bound.

With feet and hands transfix'd in pain
    He bursts our bonds in twain;
For us a healing fount He bore,
    At every bleeding pore:
The nails that hold Thee on the tree
    Bind us to that and Thee

Thy heart, now still'd by death's cold trance,
  Hath pierced the barbèd lance,
Op'ning a door to all below,
  Whence blood and water flow:
This hath the fount of cleansing shown,
  That is our heavenly crown.

Grant, Saviour, that for us below
  These fountains aye may flow,
The cup of healing here to prove,
  The cup of bliss above;
Then we will ever sing Thy praise
  Through Heaven's eternal days.

AT THE MATTINS.

"When we shall see Him, there is no beauty that we
should desire Him: He is despised and rejected of men,
a Man of sorrows and acquainted with grief: and we hid
as it were our faces from Him: He was despised and we
esteemed Him not."—Is. liii.

Quæ te pro populi criminibus nova.

SAY, what strange love works Thee this sad
    unrest,
  Drives Thee, the only innocent, to die
For a poor guilty nation so unblest,
That Thou, who art the good and great High-
    Priest,
  Shouldst like a cord-bound victim, help-
    less lie?

The nails, which rend Thy bleeding feet in
      twain,
   Have the enthralling nets of Satan broke,
And let Thy people go: Thy hands, which stain,
Drop after drop, that murderous bed of pain,
   From off the captive world have shook the
      yoke.

That piercing lance hath open'd pardon's door—
   Door of that heart which never knew deceit,
Whence blood and water flow, an endless store,
Which heals, sets free, and cleanses evermore:
   O wound, that went to Pity's inmost seat!

O fountains of true life! O streams divine!
   O hallowed thresholds of that pitying breast!
Shrines of that sacred heart, O sheltering mine
Op'd in the smitten rock, where we, that pine
   O'ercome with sinful shame, may hide
      and rest.

Again that Cross we plead, to Him we fly—
   O Father, when our crimes provoke Thee,
      when
Thy thunder is against us lifted high,
Look on His bleeding wounds, and pass us by,
   And for His sake spare Thou us once again.

'Mid wounds alone and crosses here we know
   That we can enter into Thy dear love,
And have our joy in the Eternal now;
Thee with the Son and Spirit praise below,
   Thee with the Son and Spirit praise above.

On Passion Sunday.

Or, the Fifth Sunday in Lent.

AT THE FIRST VESPERS.

"Who in the days of His flesh, when He had offered up prayers and supplications with strong crying and tears unto Him that was able to save Him from death, and was heard in that He feared."—*Heb.* v.

Fando quis audivit, Dei.

Who hath believed our report? to whom
Hath Thine arm been reveal'd, Incarnate Lord?
    Reason confounded stands,
    And Faith silent and mute.

O holy Lamb, slain ere the world was made,
And hast Thou from Thy Father's bosom come,
    Thyself the sacrifice
    Dimly shadow'd of old!

But why thus laid upon the cold dank ground,
Oh, why that look of fearful agony,
    While on Thy wan worn frame
    Thy blood stands, drop by drop!

It is the mighty anguish of Thy soul,
And horror at the weight of others' crimes,
    To bear Thy Father's wrath,
    And terrors of the lost.

It is the proffered cup Thy soul affrights :
Ah ! If it be that Thou drink not the whole,
    We everlastingly
    Must drink, and suck the dregs !

But Love doth master terror's agony :
Love strong in death, and His blest Father's
        will ;
    Calmly He yields Himself
    To darkness and to death.

And now unto the scourge, the twinèd thorn,
The rough rude mockery, and torturing tree,
    A lamb-like victim meek,
    He bows His holy head.

Glory to God, His only Son who gave,
The Son who died, a living sacrifice,
    And Spirit who came down
    To light the altar flame.

AT MIDNIGHT.

"I heard the defaming of many, fear on every side. Report, say they, and we will report it. All my familiars watched for my halting, saying, Peradventure he will be enticed, and we shall prevail against him, and we shall take our revenge on him. But the Lord is with me as a mighty terrible One."—*Jerem.* xx.

Opprobriis, Jesu, satur.

Up that dark hill funereal, faint with ill,
True Isaac, sinking 'neath that tree of pain,
    That dark funereal hill,
    Thou climbest to be slain.

Thy tender hands were torn unpityingly,
Thy tender feet with fangs of iron driven;
    Thou art uplifted high—
    Oh, sight for earth and heaven!

"Thy will, Eternal Father, Thine be done,"
    O, inconceived charity,
    That gave the guiltless Son
    For guilty foes to die.

From that Thy bleeding side, those bleeding
    hands,
Must the foul world be cleans'd — it needs
    must be;
    For Justice so demands,
    And Mercy grants the plea.

Else that dread bond must aye on us remain;
But from Thy Cross extending to Thy throne
        Now binds a peaceful chain,
        The earth and heavens in one.

Glory to Him, who gave His Son to die,
Him, who for us a willing victim dies,
        And Spirit, ever nigh,
        Who fired the sacrifice.

AT THE MATTINS.

"They had devised devices against me, saying, Let us destroy the tree with the fruit thereof, and let us cut him off from the land of the living, that his name may be no more remembered."—*Jerem.* xi.

Dum, Christe, confixus cruci.

O THOU, that nail'd upon the bleeding tree,
Breathest Thy soul away, let us draw nigh,
And hang our weary hearts and eyes on Thee.

To look on Thee in Thy sore agony
Shall heal that Serpent's wounds that long hath
        strove,
And fill'd our veins with death. While Thou
        dost die,

We from Thy throes are born to life above :
'Tis thus Thou build'st Thy martyrs, and 'tis
        thus
That Faith herself doth anchor on Thy love.

While with Thine arms outstretch'd, bleeding
    and bare,
As to Thy throne of Godhead, Thou to Thee
Dost draw the big round world, let us draw near

And, clinging at the foot of that dread tree,
Beneath Thy wither'd frame and bleeding side,
Hide ourselves, and look up, dear Lord, to Thee.

That only hope of refuge, only pride
Of a lost world, oh, may it o'er us reign,
And in the fountain of our hearts abide.

Glory to Thee, Eternal Victim slain,
Father who gave, and Holy Paraclete,
As was, and is, and shall for aye remain.

AT THE VESPERS.

"Remember that I stood before Thee to speak good for
them, and to turn away Thy wrath from them."—*Jer.* xviii.

Vexilla Regis prodeunt.

Is this the standard of a king?
    It is the Cross, that sign of myst'ery,
The wood on which, like some accursèd thing,
    The world's great Maker deign'd to die,
Where He sustain'd the lance's iron wound,
Whence for our souls water and blood abound.

Wonderful tree, and from old time
　　Oft in mysterious measures darkly sung,
On which, as on a purple throne sublime,
　　The dreadful King of Glory hung :
O precious wood, thou art surpassing fair ;
Blest tree, found meet those sacred limbs to
　　　　bear.

Blessèd, and blessèd-making tree,
　　From what most noble stock didst thou arise,
That thou should'st touch those limbs, the
　　　　bearer be
　　Of Him, the mighty sacrifice,
Who, drop by drop, the world's price told that
　　　　day,
And rescued from hell's jaws the living prey.

Hail, holy Cross, sole refuge, hail !
　　At this the season of our suffering Lord ;
In our grief's bitter waters so prevail,
　　That they to us may health afford :
So may devotion gain a holier mind,
And penitence therein may pardon find.

All love, all power, all praise, and might,
　　All worship, and all adoration be
To Him, who veil'd His own essential light,
　　And hung on the accursèd tree,
With Father and with Spirit, ever blest,
May on our souls Thy shadow ever rest.

The Virgin Mary at the Cross.

" What thing shall I liken to thee, O daughter of Jerusalem?
what shall I equal to thee that I may comfort thee, O virgin
daughter of Zion? for thy breach is great, like the sea : who
can heal thee ? "—*Isaiah xl.*

Illæsa te puerpera.

Not a parent's stern control,
    Not a mother's pang was thine,
    O'er thy Holy Child Divine,
But a sword shall pierce thy soul.

When He gave, with dying brow,
    Thee another son's to be,—
    Gave another son to thee,—
'Tis that pang is on thee now.

But we see no rended hair,
    And we hear no wailing cry,—
    All is silent agony,—
'Tis a mother's grief is there.

Praise to Thee, the Virgin-born,—
    Three in One for evermore,—
    To the Father of the poor,
And the Friend of them that mourn.

In the Paschal Season.

UNTIL THE ASCENSION.

AT MIDNIGHT.

"The Lord is King, and hath put on glorious apparel; the Lord hath put on His apparel, and girded Himself with strength."—Ps. xciii.

Adeste, cœlitum chori.

ANGELS come, on joyous pinion,
   Down the Heaven's melodious stair;
Triumphing o'er death's dominion,
   Up to this our lower air,
      Christ is rising,
   And doth burst the sepulchre.

All in vain the posted station
   Of the armèd soldiery,—
All in vain the faithless nation
   Sets the seal and watches nigh;
      Ye need not fear,
   None shall reach where He doth lie!

He Himself, from sleep awaking,
   Who spontaneous bears the gloom,
Through your seals, and without breaking,

Shall come forth and leave the tomb;
        Death cannot hold
    Him born of a Virgin's womb.

When His heart stern death was rending,
    They cried out, "Thy death-bed leave,
" And from off Thy Cross descending,
    " We will upon Thee believe : "
        To death resign'd,
    He would suffer no reprieve.

No, He hath not thence descended,
    Or ye would for ever grieve,
But from death He hath ascended,
    Will ye not in Him believe ?
        'Tis He alone
    Can your chains of death relieve.

Lord, with Thee in daily dying
    May we die, and with Thee rise ;
And on earth, ourselves denying,
    Have our hearts within the skies,
        To sing our God,
    Three in One, sole good and wise.

AT THE MATTINS.

"The God of peace, that brought again from the dead our Lord Jesus (that great Shepherd of the sheep,) through the blood of the everlasting covenant, make you perfect in every good work to do His will, working in you that which is well-pleasing in His sight."—*Heb.* xiii.

Aurora lucis dum novæ.

THE new morn has risen,
From the tomb's murky prison,
Go, sound the trumpet forth, and the immortal
jubilee.
The Lamb, from the skies,
Hath made the sacrifice,
Rend away the temple veil, and ope the
sanctuary.

The seed laid on earth
Hath burst to glorious birth,
Amid her empty shrouds the widowed grave
sits desolate.
A power hath shook the tomb,
Quickening earth's secret womb—
God Himself hath burst the way, and oped the
massy gate.

Hence all flesh which hath died
With Him, the Crucified,
In His own glory shall arise, crown'd with
transcendent dowers;

Then with Thee let us die,
That we may rise on high,
Where Thou lead'st forth the way to the
immortal towers.

Then let us praises sing
To our victorious King,
Who, dying, conquer'd death, and oped our
starry home;
With Father of all might,
And Spirit, fount of light,
Reveal'd in the Eternal Son, who triumph'd
o'er the tomb.

AT THE VESPERS.

" When this mortal shall have put on immortality, then shall
be brought to pass the saying that is written, Death is swal-
lowed up in victory. O death, where is thy sting? O grave,
where is thy victory? "—1 Cor. xv.

Forti tegente brachio.

Bound by a holy charm,
    We pass'd through raging sea,
And 'neath a mighty arm
    Burst chains of slavery.

Let us His praise unfold,
    Who our Avenger came;
And, robed in pureness, hold
    The festal of the Lamb!

He for our souls did bleed;
  Oh then, in holy love,
Upon Him let us feed,
  And live to God above !

Christ is our sacrifice,
  The Lamb come down from high;
Death's angel dread descries
  His blood, and passes by.

O Victim, worthy Heaven,
  Of death the victory;
Who chains of hell hath riven,
  And borne her gates away !

From jaws of the dark tomb
  He bursts into the light,
And opes beyond the gloom
  The heavenly infinite.

Grant us with Thee to die,
  That we with Thee may rise,
And build our home on high,
  On Thee beyond the skies.

Praise Father, praise the Son,
  Who leads to starry homes;
Praise Spirit, Three in One,
  Who as our Guardian comes.

AT THE COMPLINE.

"Who hath delivered us from the power of darkness, and hath translated us into the kingdom of His dear Son." Coloss. i.

Jesu, Redemptor sæculi.

THOU, who to save
The world didst die, and then Thy breath
Resume, to vanquish gloomy death,
    And kill the grave.

O'er all below
Night reigns; our eyes are weigh'd with
    sleep ;
O, from the wiles and watchings keep
    Of the great foe.

May rest, which lays
Care's lid, and labour's brow doth slake,
Quicken our hearts, more fresh to wake
    Unto Thy praise.

O, be it given
With Thee to die, on earth to love
The better things which are above,
    And dwell in Heaven.

And now all praise
To Father and to Holy Ghost,
And Him who leads His ransom'd host
    On starry ways.

On the Ascension.

AT THE FIRST AND SECOND VESPERS.

"Lift up your heads, O ye gates, and be ye lift up, ye everlasting doors: and the King of Glory shall come in. Who is the King of Glory? It is the Lord strong and mighty, even the Lord mighty in battle."—Ps. xxiv.

Opus peregisti tuum.

Blest Saviour, now Thy work is done
  Of death and hell the victory;
And Thou ascended to put on
  The glories of eternity.

Now borne upon a glittering cloud,
  Thou seest afar earth's little bound;
While, following, flock a happy crowd,
  Their Saviour and their King around.

'Mid wondering angels, without end,
  Th' eternal doors are open wide;
While Man and God Thou dost ascend,
  To set Thee at Thy Father's side.

Our One High-Priest, our Advocate,
  Our Intercessor there on high,
Offering for us without the gate
  The blood of boundless Charity.

Thence Thou Thy bride dost here adorn,
  And cherish her in her unrest,
And she, when harass'd and forlorn,
  Reclines upon Thy faithful breast.

Thou midst her conflicts art at hand,
  Thou o'er her head dost hold Thy shield,
By Thee alone she is sustain'd,
  By Thee hath power her arms to wield.

Where Thou our Head art gone before,
  Do Thou to Thee the body draw—
On ways, where Thine own steps of yore
  Have trod Thine own life-giving Law.

Now to the Father let us sing,
  And Holy Spirit, unto Thee,
And to our Heaven-ascended King
  Who captive led captivity.

AT MIDNIGHT.

" Behold, one like the Son of Man came with the clouds
of Heaven, and came to the Ancient of Days, and they
brought Him near before Him. And there was given Him
dominion, and glory, and a kingdom."—*Dan.* vii.

Promissa, tellus, concipe gaudia.

AND now, glad earth, take up thine Hallelujah,
  Bright day, spousal of Heaven and earth, all
      hail :
Averted is the wrath of dread Jehovah,
  The Mediator gone within the veil !

O Christ, put on Thee now Thy hard-earn'd
        glory,
  Conqueror of hell and death, as is most meet,
Go on, and reign, for to all time before Thee
  Thy kingdom lies, the world is 'neath Thy
        feet.

And who are ye, where your Lord hath as-
        cended,
  Gazing where on Heaven's vault His foot-
        steps burn ?
As He ascends with golden clouds attended,
  So as a dreadful Judge shall He return.

O Christ, upon Thy Father's right-hand sitting,
  Make us partakers of Thy triumph now,
Fierce is the warfare, but it were most fitting,
  While Thou dost lead, that we o'ercome
        the foe.

Glory to God the Father, into Heaven
  Who hath receiv'd the hostage of our peace,
And to the Spirit Divine be glory given,
  And glory to the Son, our sure release.

AT THE MATTINS.

"Who being the brightness of His glory, and the express image of His person, and upholding all things by the word of His power, when He had by Himself purged our sins, sat down on the right hand of the majesty on high."—*Heb.* i.

Jesu, nostra Redemptio.

Jesu, who our redemption art,
God, Maker of all things, ere time began,
In the world's evening seen as Son of Man,
  Sole love and light of the sad heart.

What tender pity won Thee so
That Thou shouldst take on Thee our sinful
      stains,
And bear the very worst of dying pains,
  That we might 'scape the penal woe.

To rescue thence Thy captive band
Thou went'st below, and through th' infernal
      bars
Girt with Thy ransom'd, like a robe of stars,
  Didst sit down at Thy Father's side.

Let that dear pity spare us still,
And so, by sparing, overcome our sin,

That here Thy blissful countenance may win
　Our yearning hearts, hereafter fill.

　Thou art the Crown for evermore
Which doth await Thy faithful soldier's brow :
In Thee be all our peace and glory now,
　In Thee upon the eternal shore.

On the Octave of the Ascension.

AT THE FIRST VESPERS.

"The hand of the Lord shall be known towards His servants, and His indignation towards His enemies: for behold, the Lord will come with fire."—*Isaiah* lxvi.

Felix dies mortalibus.

BLEST day, when doom'd to die no more,
Our Saviour oped the starry way,
  Through Heaven's eternal door,
  That had been closed from aye!

Our Head hath pierced the skies, and we
The body left, but not alone,
  If one in charity,
  In glory shall be one.

Yea, He hath gone, but still is nigh;
Unseen, in Spirit present still,
  Doth every limb supply,
  And all the body fill.

But, oh, that day, when from His throne,
Th' avenger of our crimes to be,
  The Heavens shall let Him down
  In terror's panoply!

He, once arraign'd as criminal,
The Judge returns, and from afar
  Sitting on high shall call
  His judges to the bar.

He died —that He from death might save
What vengeance shall for them remain,
  To whom a Saviour's grave,
  The blood of God is vain!

Then let the guilty now come forth,
Ere love in terror disappears,
  And flames of wakening wrath
  Extinguish with our tears.

We Thee, who as our Judge shalt come,
With Father and with Spirit praise,
  Thee, who shalt bring our doom
  For the eternal days.

AT MIDNIGHT.

"When the Son of Man shall come in His glory, and all
the holy Angels with Him, then shall He sit upon the
throne of His glory: and before Him shall be gathered
all nations."—*Matt.* xxv.

Sensus quis horror percutit?

WHAT is this horror!
The sky is rended,
Christ sits,—and all o'er
Angels are hurrying,—all is ended!

The trump hath sounded,—
Death's warrant is past,—
The dead, surrounded,
Hasten to judgment: 'tis come at last.

At His own right hand
He hath set His own,
Alas, that dark band,—
The Shepherd too well His sheep hath known.

By the Judge's side
They are set on high,
Who did poor abide,
And fled to Him here in His poverty.

The Cross shines to view,
In the opening skies,
To Gentile and Jew,
Dreadful or glad to all gazing eyes.

Trembling and sighing
They see Him they wounded,
There is now no dying,
For them whom His look hath aye confounded.

Before that dread day,
When all is over,
While yet we may,
Lord, to ourselves our sins discover.

To Thee, who shalt come
At the end of days
With our endless doom,
To God, Three and One, be endless praise.

AT THE MATTINS AND VESPERS.

"As it is appointed unto men once to die, but after this
the judgment; so Christ was once offered to bear the
sins of many; and unto them that look for Him shall
He appear the second time without sin unto salvation."
Heb. ix.

Nobis Olympo redditus.

THOU, who dost build for us on high
A house beyond the crystal sky,
  Lead us to Thee above,
    With cords of love.

Thou in whom dwelleth every good,
Thyself shalt be the soul's abode,
  Waking from life's brief night
    To endless light.

Then shall we see Thee as Thou art,
Thy countenance pure, nor fear to part,
  To love Thee and adore
    For evermore.

If Thou dost love us, leave us not;
But send down from that pure calm spot,
  Pledge of adopting love,
    That fostering Dove.

Thou who shalt come our Judge to be,
Jesu, the glory be to Thee,
  With God and Spirit pure
    Aye to endure !

On Whitsun=eve.

AT MIDNIGHT.

"Like as the hart desireth the water-brooks; so longeth
my soul after Thee, O God."—*Psalm xlii*.

O Christe qui noster poli.

O Thou, gone up, our harbinger,
  To Heaven's dread palaces,
Look on us lying helpless here,
  And lift us to the skies.

May holy love the stair supply
  To those pure joys divine,
Which, undiscern'd by nature's eye,
  In Faith's true mirror shine.

Where God doth His tried children own,
  And gives Him to the blest,
He, all in all, their toils doth crown,
  And is Himself their rest.

Thy grace alone to Thee can lead,
  And place us near Thy throne,
Do Thou, to help us in our need,
  Send down Thy Holy One.

Praise Him who sits at God's right hand,
  Praise Father, as most meet,
And to all time, in every land,
  Praise the dread Paraclete!

AT THE MATTINS.

"Thy counsel, O Lord, who hath known, except Thou
give wisdom and send Thy Holy Spirit from above? for so
the ways of them which lived on the earth were reformed,
and men were taught the things that are pleasing unto
Thee."—*Wisdom* ix.

Supreme Rector cœlitum.

DREAD King, to whom the angelic hosts do
    cry,
Who tramplest death 'neath Thy victorious
    feet,
And op'st a path unto the glorious sky,
Mark'd by Thy blood! From the eternal seat,
Where Thou, with the life-giving Paraclete,
Sitt'st by Thy Father's side, look on us now,
Nor leave us comfortless: let our wants meet
Thy pitying eyes! Thy covenanted bow
Is left upon Thy path, and marks the clouds
    below.

Thou didst give birth to us with piercing
    throes,
And direst travail pains, while the dark tide
Of woes o'erwhelm'd Thee, and brought
    death's repose;

Then the rude lance open'd Thy bleeding
    side,
And thence was taken Thine own spotless
    Bride,
The Mother of us all.   From Thy calm shore
Send forth Thy Spirit of Truth, who shall
    abide :
Wash'd in Thy blood, the Church shall Him
    adore,
And Thee and Father blest worship for ever-
    more.

On Whit-Sunday.

AT THE FIRST VESPERS.

"I will pour out My Spirit upon all flesh; and your sons
and your daughters shall prophesy, your old men shall dream
dreams, and your young men shall see visions."—*Joel* ii.

Veni, superne Spiritus.

Come, Spirit from above!
Earth, wash'd with blood of Him that
       died,
  With eyes of awe and love,
Awaits Thee, calm and purified.

  Come, in the holy Name
Of Him, who hath gone up on high :
  With Thy Baptism of flame
Cleanse Thou our hearts, and sanctify.

  A Father, gone from sight,
We mourn ; pity our orphanhood,
  And with Thy gentle might
Heal us, and help us to be good.

  The lesson His sweet care
Forbore to teach th' untutor'd heart,
  As yet unschool'd to bear,
With Thy life-giving dew impart.

The things by seer of old
Darkly and dim in shadow seen,
   Nations come to behold;
For Thou hast rent the veil between.

Thy blest anointing give;
The letters, now on mute heart writ,
   Then shall come forth and live,
By Thy celestial brightness lit.

Throughout eternity,
Unto the Father and the Son,
   And Spirit, glory be;
The Spirit, binding Three in One.

AT MIDNIGHT.

"This shall be the covenant that I will make with the house of Israel, after those days, saith the Lord; I will put My law in their inward parts, and write it in their hearts."
Jerem. xxxi.

Inter sulphurei fulgura turbinis.

'MID dread whirlwinds wheeling round,
Lightning fires, and trumpet's sound,
From dark Sinai's dread profound,
Thy wrath-denouncing Law went forth in
   terror by.

Thus to faithless hearts were spoken
Terrors of Thy statutes broken:
What avails the dreadful token,
And dark portending signs of awful majesty?

Round the smoking mountain's base
(Awful sight!) the chosen race,
E'en now, in Jehovah's place,
Worship an idol foul and molten Deity.

Without Thee such man at best;
Wrap our hearts with Thine own vest,
Take the iron from our breast,
That we may hear Thy voice and ever feel
　　Thee nigh.

Praise the Father and the Son,
And the Spirit, Three in One,
Him, from whom a heart is won,
To love Thy law, and, with responsive feet,
　　comply.

AT THE MATTINS.

"He that hath an ear, let him hear what the Spirit saith
unto the Churches."—Rev. ii.

Audimur ; almo Spiritus.

Now our prayers are heard on high,
　　And 'mid mortal men unblest,
The good Comforter is nigh,
　　Coming from the Father's breast.

What mysterious sight and sound
　　Of our God the coming speaks!
Like a rushing wind profound,
　　All the house His presence shakes.

Like a fiery shower it falls
  All the hallow'd guests among,
Upon each within the walls
  Sitting like a flaming tongue.

While the bright and lambent blaze
  Plays their unharm'd heads around,
It hath gone, with piercing rays,
  To their deepest hearts profound.

All aghast the nations throng,
  While with other tongues they name
Things that unto Heaven belong,
  And whate'er they speak is flame.

Lo, again, O sight of fear,
  For the hearer hath a tongue;
Of new prophets, while they hear,
  Hath another harvest sprung.

Praise to Father, and to Son,
  And to Thee, the Holy One,
By whose awful breath divine
  Our dull spirits burn and shine.

AT THE THIRD HOUR.

"The Spirit of Truth; whom the world cannot receive, because it seeth Him not, neither knoweth Him: but ye know Him; for He dwelleth with you, and shall be in you."—*John* xiv.

Veni Creator Spiritus.

COME Thou Creating Spirit blest,
    And be our guest,
And fill the hearts, which Thou hast made,
    With Thy sweet shade.
Thou, who art called the Paraclete,
    From Thy blest seat,
The living Fount of light and love,
    Come from above.
Thou that in seven-fold power dost stand
    At God's right hand,
And layest on the untutor'd tongue
    The Spirit's song,
Unto our senses light impart,
    Love to our heart;
And may our flesh's infirmity
    Be strong in Thee,
May the foe's assaultings cease,
    And grant Thy peace;
That, treading in Thy footsteps blest,
    We may find rest.
May we by Thee the Father know,
    And Son below,
And Thee, the Spirit come from both,
    Trust, nothing loth!

To Father, Son, and Holy One,
    Praise aye be done,
From whose sweet effluence Divine
    We too may shine.

AT THE SECOND VESPERS.

"According to His mercy He saved us, by the washing
of regeneration, and renewing of the Holy Ghost: which He
shed on us abundantly through Jesus Christ our Saviour,
that, being justified by His grace, we should be made heirs
according to the hope of eternal life."—*Titus* iii.

Quo vos Magistri gloria, quo salus.

WHERE thy Master's glory
    Calls thee forth abroad,
And Heaven's light before thee
    Opens all the road,
Go, little band, to bear high behests of God.

See the harvest springing,
    Thrice a thousand souls,
Which our God is bringing,
    And His hand controls,
From every peopled land where the sunshine
    rolls.

Hearts with sorrow turning,
    And compunctious throes,

With dread hope are burning—
    Sion's fountain flows,
To wash their guilty stains, and they find
    repose.

Nor shall Canaan's border
    The great flood confine,
Where Heaven's golden warder
    Shoots his glowing line,
Far mightier than his fires pass the rays divine.

To their fall declining
    Thousand temples nod,
Where through clouds is shining
    The true light of God,
And towers of heathen strength 'neath their
    feet are trod.

Lo, a new creation,
    Rising into view,
And in order'd station,
    Drinking heavenly dew :
Good Spirit, with Thy love make Thou me anew.

Praise to Holy Spirit,
    To Father and to Son,
By whom we inherit
    The Eternal One,
With hearts woke from the dead by the living
    Sun.

AT THE COMPLINE.

"If the ministration of death, written and engraven in stones, was glorious, so that the children of Israel could not stedfastly behold the face of Moses for the glory of his countenance, which glory was to be done away: how shall not the ministration of the Spirit be rather glorious." 2 Cor. iii.

Adsis superne Spiritus.

HAIL Father of the poor, and Friend benign,
    Immortal Spirit Divine,
From out Thine own prolific bosom pour
Thy promised blessings on the barren earth,
    Which gladdeneth at Thy birth.

Here, where night comes from Heaven's alter-
    nate door
To muffle up the blooming eye of day,
    With uncreated ray
Shine forth, cease not to shine,
Shine in our hearts, good Spirit, evermore.

Thou of the inner heart art guest and friend,
Thou of all labours art the sweet repose;
    Thou op'st the fount of woes,
The cup of sorrow at Thy bidding flows;
But Thou dost Thy pure joys divinely blend,
And as the blended streams flow forth apace,
    Dost o'er them pitying bend.

Thou art the fount of grace :
Grant us with holy hardness to contend,
To conquer and to win th' immortal end,
     Which is to see Thy face,
 And ever sing in the undefilèd place,
The Father, Son, and Thee, the Spirit benign,
       Bath'd in whose fires divine,
E'en our dull hearts may catch the light and
              shine.

On Trinity Sunday.

AT THE FIRST VESPERS.

"O the depth of the riches both of the wisdom and knowledge of God! how unsearchable are His judgments, and His ways past finding out!"—*Rom.* xi.

Ter sancte, ter potens Deus.

THRICE holy, thrice Almighty Three,
Incomprehended Trinity.
 O uncreated Light all One,
 O never ending, ne'er begun,
 Thrice beatific Union!
 O ever very Unity,
 O ever triune Verity,
 O all-upholding Charity!
Where the thickest clouds surround
The unapproachèd ray is found,
Angels, bending to the ground,
 Trembling glow, nor dare to know
Th' ineffable and dread profound.
Born of Thee, we Thee confess,
All-perfect in Thy blessedness:

Faith, kindling into charity,
Hath dared to raise her thoughts to Thee,
And tastes of what herself shall be.
Father, give us to do what Thou
        Wouldst have done:
What Thou dost teach give us to know,
        Holy Son;
And to approve what Thou dost love,
        Holy One.

AT MIDNIGHT.

"There are Three that bear record in Heaven, the Father,
the Word, and the Holy Ghost; and these Three are One."—
John v.

Sublime Numen, ter potens, ter maximum.

ALL-good, all-great, all-mighty, Three in One,
The Father, and the Spirit, and the Son—
Ineffable mysterious union!

Sublimest Name! all-holy, boundless rays,
Of unborn light encircle all Thy ways;
All things created labour Thee to praise.

Father, Thou art the inexhaustive well,
Where the mysterious Trinity doth dwell—
Incomprehensible, unspeakable!

All One in substance, One in Majesty;
All One in substance, but in person Three;
The Son of Thee is born: the Spirit free

From both proceeds, with both is glorified:
The Father in the Son doth aye reside;
The Son doth in the Father aye abide;

And each is in the Holy Spirit found;
The Holy Spirit doth in both abound:
Nothing the centre is, and nought the bound.

None after in the Three, and none before,—
Shall be as they are now, and were of yore,
Equal in power and Godhead evermore.

Praise equal to the Father aye we raise,
And to the Son praise equal be always;
And always to the Spirit equal praise. Amen

AT THE MATTINS.

"Blessing, and glory, and wisdom, and thanksgiving, and
honour, and power, and might, be unto our God, for ever
and ever. Amen."—Rev. vii.

O luce quæ tuâ lates.

O THOU, who hidden art in Thine own light,
Blessèd, for ever blessèd Trinity,
　　We Thy great name confess,
　　And trembling seek to know!

O Father, holiest of most holy, Thou!
Thou God of very God, eternal Son!
　　And Thou, in chain of Love,
　　Great Spirit, binding all!

The Father doth Himself behold entire,
From Him the offspring is coeval born :
   And from both, in life-giving love,
   God doth Himself proceed.

In God the Son the Father is entire ;
The Son entire in God the Father is ;
   In Father and the Son
   The Spirit is entire.

Such as the Son, e'en such the Spirit is,
And such as either such the Father is ;
   In Verity Three-One,
   Three-One in Charity.

Hymns on the Holy Eucharist.

"I appoint unto you a kingdom, as My Father hath appointed unto Me, that ye may eat and drink at My table in My kingdom."—*Luke* xxii.

Sacris solemniis juncta sint gaudia.

SOLEMN rites arise to view,
   Dread our joy to-day;
All things are becoming new,
   Old things pass away:
New must all things hence proceed,
   Heart, and tongue, and deed;
From the Spirit's inmost shrine,
   Awful, deep, divine.

When on that immortal even,
   Ever known again,
The unleavened bread was given,
   And the lamb was slain:
And, as holy writ hath told,
   In dim type of old,
Ate they the dread sacrifice,
   Girt for great emprize:

To each body, to each soul,
   Gave He then the bread;
On Himself in spirit whole,
   Each and all were fed:

Then the cup which souls shall save
  Unto all He gave;
Cup of everlasting bliss,
  " Drink ye all of this !"

Awful rite, angelic food,
  By which dead men live;
Christ's Priests to the multitude,
  He to them doth give.
Miracle, o'erwhelming thought,
  Ever newly-wrought;
Man, a poor vile slave—made free—
  Eateth of Divinity!

Triune God, as we adore,
  So be Thou our Guest;
On Thy paths for evermore
  Lead us to Thy rest.
From our gloom to infinite
  Everlasting light;
From our loud tumultuous round
  To Thy calm profound.

———

" I am the Bread of Life: He that cometh to Me shall
never hunger; and He that believeth on Me shall never
thirst."—John vi.

Verbum supernum prodiens.

THE Word, who ever sits at God's right hand,
From the bright houses of eternity,
    Went forth unto His work
    At solemn eventide.

As time drew near that His own chosen friend
Should yield Him up to envious enemies,
    He gave Himself, e'en like
    An offer'd sacrifice,—

Gave Himself to His own with His own hands—
A twofold offering of both flesh and blood—
    That so the double gift
    Might the whole man sustain.

When born, He was Himself their guide and
       friend,
When eating with them, was Himself their
       food;
    In dying, paid their price,
    Reigning, is their reward.

O Lord, who didst a willing victim die,
Open for us the long-closed doors of Heaven—
    Wars on all sides oppress,
    Strengthen and grant us aid.

Thou, who Thy sheep dost feed with Thine
       own flesh;
Good Shepherd, unto Thee, with Father blest,
    And Spirit, evermore
    All glory be to Thee.

Pange lingua gloriosi.

SPEAK, O tongue, the body broken,
  Given to be the spirit's food;
And the word almighty spoken,
  Which hath turn'd the wine to blood,
Of the King the awful token,
  And celestial brotherhood.

Born for us, and for us given,
  Of a Virgin undefil'd,
Scattering wide the seeds of Heaven,
  Sojourn'd He in this world's wild;
And on that remember'd even,
  His appointed course fulfill'd.

Meekly to the law complying,
  He had finish'd its commands,
And to them at supper lying,
  Gave Himself, with His own hands;
A memorial of His dying,
  Hence to be unto all lands.

'Tis His Word to our receiving
  Makes the bread His Flesh to be,
And the wine, our sins relieving,
  Blood, that flow'd upon the tree;
Though not seeing, yet believing,
  Take we the great mystery.

To our smitten Rock thus fleeing,
  Drink we the new Covenant ;
Which to ancient types agreeing,
  To the latest time is sent :
Still believing, though not seeing,
  Take we this dread Sacrament.

Now all might and adoration
  To the dreadful Trinity ;
Honour, worship, and salvation,
  And immortal glory be :
Coeternal Three, in station,
  And in power coequal Three.

"I am the Bread of Life: he that cometh to Me shall never hunger; and he that believeth on Me shall never thirst."—John vi.

Adoro te supplex, latens Deitas.

O DREADFUL, unapproachèd Deity,
Who 'neath these symbols giv'st Thyself to me;
The heart of hearts prostrate before Thee falls,
And cannot reach Thee; contemplation fails,
In dread amazement lost: I hear Thy words,
"This is My Body," which the Son of God,
The Word of Truth hath spoken; I believe,
And know no more: Thou art Thyself the
  Truth.
Upon Thy Cross Thy manhood hung to view,
Thy Godhead was conceal'd from earthly eyes:
Thy Body here we see not, but believe.

And I would on Thee gaze, and make the prayer
Of the poor penitent thief,—Remember me !
Though I behold Thee not, nor feel Thy wounds,
Like Thomas—I would hide mine eyes, and cry,
Thou art my Lord and God ! Make me believe
And love Thee ; make me to believe Thee more,
And more to love, and have my hope in Thee.
O dread Memorial, only Sacrifice,
True living Bread, the Bread that gives true
    life,
Make my soul taste Thee, feed on Thee, and
    live.
O Fount of purity ! Jesu, my Lord,
Unclean—unclean am I, make Thou me clean
With Thine own blood ; of which one little drop
Can cleanse the guilty world of all her sin.
O Thou, whom I behold beneath the veil,
Grant one thing unto me, for which I thirst,
Suppliant I pray Thee, that I may behold
Thy gracious countenance without the veil ;
And, when I see Thy glory, may be blest.

PERSONS AND EVENTS

RECORDED IN

HOLY SCRIPTURE.

On the Blessed Virgin Mary.

"He that is mighty hath done to me great things,
and holy is His name."—*Luke* i.

Ut sol decoro lumine.

As the sun
  O'er misty shrouds,
When he walks
  Upon the clouds ;

Or as when
  The moon doth rise,
And refreshes
  All the skies ;

Or as when
  The lily flower
Stands amid
  The vernal bower ;

Or the water's
  Glassy face
Doth reflect
  The starry space;

Thus above
  All mothers shone
The mother of
  The Blessed One.

" In Thee shall all the families of the earth be
blessed."—*Gen.* xii.

Unus bonorum fons, Deus, omnium.

O THOU sole Fountain of all good,
How hast Thou from Thy dark abode
Open'd Thine hand! Thine Israel own'd,
Thy handmaid with Thy bounty crown'd.

As on a rugged thorn the rose
Though hostile briers round her close,
Yet o'er a thousand armèd spears
Her gentleness in beauty rears.

Thus meekly, mid our ruin'd race,
Hath grace found out a dwelling-place,
And, through that maiden-mother given,
Appear'd the loveliness of Heaven.

All glory to the Eternal Three,
Who, pitying man's poor destiny,
Have sent the pledge of mercy down
To herald Him, the Holy One.

On the Conversion of St. Paul.

AT THE FIRST VESPERS.

"Benjamin shall raven as a wolf: in the morning he shall devour the prey, and at night he shall divide the spoil."— *Genesis xlix.*

Pastore percusso minas.

The Shepherd smitten is, and, lo,
   His flock the wolf is scattering wide;
For Saul as yet doth little know
   He wounds in them a Saviour's side.

Prisons, and chains, and murderous wrath,
   He breathes, where stern religion calls,
But one soft word has crossed his path,
   And on the ground he stricken falls.

Saul, Saul, whence art thou? whither driven,
   To persecute Christ's little band?
This is to wage a war with Heaven,
   An arm almighty to withstand.

Lo, forth he spreads beseeching hands,
   Prepared beneath Christ's yoke to go,
And, trembling, asks for His commands,—
   What would'st Thou have Thy servant do?

The spoiler fierce is lying low,
  The vanquisher lies vanquishèd,
And he, who wore a threat'ning brow,
  He is himself in triumph led.

O Lord, it is Thy voice that shakes
  Great Lebanon, with matchless case
It goeth forth from Thee, and breaks
  The tall aspiring cedar-trees.

Good Shepherd, keep us as of old,
  If Thou should'st hurtful aught discern ;
And, if we wander from Thy fold,
  Again to Thee our bosoms turn.

Glory to God, both One and Three,
  Who saw us laid in dead of night,
Glory and praise be unto Thee,
  Who call'st us thence to glorious light.

AT MIDNIGHT.

"The wild boar out of the wood doth root it up: and the
wild beasts of the field devour it. Turn Thee again, Thou
God of Hosts, look down from Heaven: behold and visit
this vine."—*Psalm* lxxx.

Quos in hostes, Saule, tendis ?

WHITHER, Saul, this raging sense
  In thy bosom burning,
On defenceless innocence
  All thy fury turning ?
Other than thou hast in mind
An avenger shalt thou find.

Christ is now at hand, behold,
  Who His power defieth ?
Where is now pursuer bold ?
  On the earth he lieth :
And Christ's armèd foe e'en now
Shall as Christ's meek herald go.

He, who, filled with threatnings, sped,
  Chains and death preparing ;
By a gentle hand is led,
  With a childlike bearing ;
Like a raging wolf he came
But he goes a gentle lamb.

Lord, men's hearts in sternest mood
  Open lie before Thee ;
He who in Thy children's blood,
  Would blot out Thy glory,
With his blood shall it rehearse
Through the boundless universe.

Praise the Father, by whose might
  Life to us is given ;
And the Son, by whose blest light
  We are born to Heaven ;
And the Spirit, by whose breath
We are saved from endless death.

AT THE MATTINS.

"Nevertheless, I live, yet not I, but Christ liveth in me; and the life which I now live in the flesh, I live by the faith of the Son of God, who loved me, and gave Himself for me."— *Gal.* ii.

Quæ gloriosum tanta cælis evocat.

Lord, from out Thy glorious skies,
  Where Thy palace lies,
What cause constraining in Thine eyes
  Brings Thee again to earth?
That Thou, the Judge of endless doom,
Again should as a Saviour come,—
  What foe doth call Thee forth?

With defying mien and tread
  Hastes a warrior dread;
Afar the trembling flock is fled:
  What hand can succour lend?
With suppliant gaze beseechingly
Their eyes look up; but from the sky
  No pitying form doth bend.

Forth hath gone one awful sound,
  And the world is bound,
With Saul laid suppliant on the ground.
  At morn went forth to slay
The ravening wolf of Benjamin,
But with the sheep, when eve comes in,
  He shall divide the prey.

Through all climes His glory plant!
  Through all ages chant!
Sing praise and honour jubilant,
  As is and aye hath been!
All worship, all dominion,
To Him who all things holds in one,
  The Triune God unseen!

On the Presentation of Christ in the Temple;

OR, THE PURIFICATION. OF THE VIRGIN MARY.

AT THE FIRST VESPERS.

"Behold, I will send My messenger, and He shall prepare the way before Me; and the Lord, whom ye seek, shall suddenly come to His temple, even the Messenger of the Covenant, whom ye delight in.—Behold, He shall come, saith the Lord of Hosts."—*Mal. iii.*

Templi sacratas, pande, Sion, fores.

Sion, ope thy hallowed dome :
To His temple Christ is come ;—
Lifeless shadows, haste away,
Grace and Truth beam out to-day.

Flocks and herds shall bleed no more,—
Stanch'd the flood of reeking gore;
Lo! He comes from Heaven above,
Victim to His Father's love.

Virgin pure, thy downcast eye
Owns His hidden Godhead nigh;
Heavenly musings, all unheard,
Meetly hail the silent Word ;—

Whilst to Heaven Thy pious love
Duly vows the sacred dove,
And upon Thy bosom lies
More than dove-like sacrifice.

Sire and sister, age and youth
Kindle at the mighty truth,
And the blissful Presence own,
Panting Faith so long hath known.

Glory be to Father, Son,
And blest Spirit, Three in One.
God Triune, to Thee we raise
Faithful hearts in ceaseless praise.

AT MIDNIGHT.

"Let your loins be girded about, and your lights burning,
and ye yourselves like unto men that wait for their Lord."
—Luke xii,

Fumant sabæis templa vaporibus.

Sweet incense breathes around,
    The coming Lord to greet;
And Sion, through her sacred bound,
    Awakes her God to meet.
Arise ye then, ye wakeful quires,
And early light your altar-fires.

Let Faith, with glistening eye,
  Trim up her torch so bright;
And flame-encircled Charity
  Breathe out her glowing light:
And white-robed Innocence be there,
To pour its sweetest incense-prayer.

Why love to linger here—
  These guilty days prolong?—
More blessèd far yon dying seer;
  Be ours his parting song!
And He, whom here by faith we see,
Shall our eternal portion be.

To God, the Father, Son,
  And Spirit, glory be;
To the eternal Three in One,
  To all eternity!
Blest Trinity, to Thee we raise
Our joyous hearts in ceaseless praise.

AT THE MATTINS.

"The mystery, which hath been hid from ages and from generations, now is made manifest to His saints, to whom God would make known what is the riches of the glory of this mystery."—*Colos*. i.

Qui sacris hodie sistitur aris.

WHO now in helpless infancy
  By His own altar lies;
The ensign to the nations He,
  Descended from the skies.

The glory He of Israel's line,
Of all the world the light divine !

Above, around, their hymns of joy
  The viewless Angels sing,
And throngs, unseen by human eye,
  Adore the infant King.
The wondering parents catch the lays,
And inly breathe unconscious praise.

Scarce can the raptured spirit bear
  The Heaven-inspirèd thought :
And Hope, that many a live-long year
  The lingering Saviour sought,
Transported with the wondrous view,
Can scarce believe the vision true.

Thou, whom in trancèd ecstasy,
  The Prophets dimly scann'd,
Art now beheld by mortal eye,
  And borne by mortal hand :
And, when Thou shalt again appear,
Shalt waken every ear to hear.

Lord, when Thou art ascended high,
  And from Thy temple gone,
Let Faith her eagle-wings supply,
  And watch Thee to Thy throne,—
Her mystic touch still feel Thee here,
And in each heart Thine altar rear.

To the Eternal Father be
  Eternal praise above :
Eternal glory, Lord, to Thee,
  Pledge of that Father's love.
To Father, Son, and Spirit blest,
Coequal glory be addrest.

AT SECOND VESPERS.

"Christ being come, an High Priest of good things to
come, by a greater and more perfect tabernacle, not made
with hands, that is to say, not of this building; neither by
the blood of goats and calves, but by His own blood He
entered in once into the Holy place, having obtained
eternal redemption for us."—*Heb.* ix.

Stupete gentes, fit Deus hostia.

TREMBLE, ye Gentile lands—
  Bound in the narrow bands
Of Israel's law, the Law's dread Lord is laid ;
  Less than the least esteem'd,—
  Redeemer, yet redeem'd,
And for His sinless birth a sinner's offering
      paid.

  Matron of Israel true,
  The Mother-maid withdrew,
Nor came to worship to His temple door,—
  The Law's accustom'd days
  Restrain'd her pious praise,
Nor to His presence-court the wondrous infant
      bore.

And, lo, the threefold band,
That by yon altar stand !
Childhood, and age, and virgin purity :—
She, mother undefil'd,
And He, her Heaven-born child,
And age, at such a sight, content in peace
to die.

But, ah ! what sorrows fierce,
What sword that heart shall pierce,
Oh, born for keenest throb of deepest woe !—
See they,—old Simeon's eyes,
Another altar rise,
And from this Holy Lamb th' atoning life-blood
flow ?—

E'en now, in childhood weak,
All innocent and meek,
Death's dark wing hovers o'er His holy head :—
And soon to Manhood's bloom
His sorrowing years shall come,
And soon for guilty man His guiltless blood be
shed.

To God the Father, Son,
And Spirit, Three in One,
In union blest, one common voice we raise.
To Thee, blest Trinity,
Eternal glory be ;
Pure be our hearts, and ceaseless be our praise.

On the Annunciation of the Blessed Virgin Mary.

AT THE FIRST VESPERS.

"Sing and rejoice, O daughter of Zion; for, lo, I come,
and I will dwell in the midst of thee, saith the Lord."
—*Zech.* ii.

Hæc illa solemnis dies.

This is the festal light,
Salvation's herald bright,
When the golden sun was sent
From the crystal firmament.
We were all in ruin'd plight,
Falling on to endless night :
To take the fallen for His own,
Lo, God Himself comes down.
Who with the Eternal Father shared
    His throne,
And on His bosom lay, the Eternal Son,
He wears time's lowly weeds,
Nor scorns the Virgin's womb, the Holy
    One,—
Puts on our mortal needs,
And as our victim bleeds,
That by His guiltless blood He may atone
For all our guilty deeds.

He who fills all with His own Deity,
  Our earth hath trod,
In lineaments of poor mortality :
  To bring us back to God,
  He makes us His abode.
Then to His feet, who comes our King,
  All worship let us bring ;
Three Persons and one God let endless
  ages sing.

AT MIDNIGHT.

"The Angel came in unto her, and said, Hail, thou that art highly favoured; the Lord is with thee: blessed art thou among women."—*Luke* l.

Cœlestis ales nuntiat.

THE herald lights from Heaven on golden wing,
Announcing mysteries,—the time is come,—
And God Himself, with dread o'ershadowing,
  Doth fill the Virgin's womb.

Thee, from that wondrous and stupendous
     birth
What blessedness, O maiden, doth await,
While God, from thine own bosom brought to
     earth,
  Makes thee the heavenly gate.

Thus moulded by the Spirit's holy flame,
From thy pure virgin body, Mother-maid,
He, the sole born of Adam free from blame,
  The flesh of Christ is made.

Thus He, who, ere the course of time began,
Was food unto the heavenly habitants,
Becometh milk for babes, the food of man,
    Food temper'd to his wants.

To praise His Name, till time his course hath
    run,
To praise His Name, all worlds shall find a
    tongue ;
To praise His Name, the Father, Spirit, Son,
    Shall ever be our song.

AT THE MATTINS.

"Who being in the form of God, thought it not robbery
to be equal with God: but made Himself of no reputation,
and took upon Him the form of a servant, and was made
in the likeness of men; and was found in fashion as a
man."—*Phil. ii.*

Pulsum supernis sedibus.

Driven from their home, their pathway
    lost,
'Mid clouds that came upon the world's fair
    morn,
    By gloom and shadows cross'd,
    Wander'd a race forlorn.

There sat One o'er Heaven's highest hall,
Who in strange charity to exile went,
    Those exiles to recall
    To that His heavenly tent.

He gave Himself a staff and stay
To feeble knees, strength to the sinking soul,
 He was Himself the way,
 He was Himself the goal.

O Thou, Eternal Verity,
In fleshly veil shadowing Thyself from sight,
 Save from Faith's chasten'd eye,
 Upon us shed Thy light.

O Thou, the Father, Spirit, Son,
Who art the everlasting Prince of Peace,
 Thy praise hath ne'er begun,
 Thy praise shall never cease.

On Joseph the Husband of the Blessed Virgin Mary.

"In simplicity of heart seek the Lord; for He will be found of them that tempt Him not; and sheweth Himself unto such as do not distrust Him."—*Wisdom* i.

Quos pompa sæculi, quos opes.

Ye whom the world hath taught to see
All in her glass of vanity,
Come, here is one will school your eyes,
 Rightly their worth to prize.

His father,—though of David's line,
Of parentage august, divine,
Yet, in a workshop vile and low,
 He wiped a labourer's brow.

Himself,—though born of God on high
And equal to Heaven's Majesty,
Yet read His title written here,
 "Son of the Carpenter!"

The sinful Adam's sinless Son
The weight of crimes He had not done,
Willing He bore, to shew the path
 Where guilt may flee from wrath.

Joseph, in thy lorn poverty
Is writ a lesson clear, that we,
Though having nothing, yet have all
  If Christ be at our call.

To God the Father praise be given,
To Spirit praise, who dwells in Heaven,
And praise to Him who became poor
  That we might find the door.

St. Philip and St. James's Day.

AT THE FIRST VESPERS.

"Their seed shall be known among the Gentiles, and their offspring among the people; all that see them shall acknowledge them, that they are the seed which the Lord hath blessed."—Isaiah lxi.

Dum morte victor obruiâ.

When from Death's chambers Christ triumphant rose,
To you His glorious form did He disclose;
Ye watch'd Him laid in the cold-bosom'd
    grave,—
Ye witness'd thence His rising strong to save :
    Whom 'twas given above the rest
    Round His person to be blest,
    His divinest ways beholding,
    When, celestial things unfolding,
He of the Kingdom spoke that should arise,
    And His death-agonies.

Ah, love shrinks back to hear of His sad pains,
Needs must He die that He may burst Death's
    chains ;
He dies, for very man the earth He trod ;
He rose, to shew that He is very God.

Train us, Lord, and teach us so
That we may the Father know,
Till to the Faith-cleans'd eye is given
Mysteries to read of Heaven;
Give us to know what is from sight conceal'd,
And love what is reveal'd.

Lord, grant us here daily with Thee to die,
Where all vexation is and vanity,
That we on earth from earthly things may
    rise,
And have with Thee our life beyond the skies.
And for ever sing of Thee,
Holy, holy, holy Three,
Never ending, ne'er begun,
Father, Spirit, holy Son,
Who hath burst our prison-bars,
And leads us to the stars.

———

AT MIDNIGHT.

"He stretched forth His hand toward His disciples, and
said, Behold, My mother and My brethren! For whosoever
shall do the will of My Father which is in Heaven, the
same is My brother, and sister, and mother."—*Matt.* xii.

Prædicta Christi mors adest.

Now the hour is drawing near
    Which your Master shall remove;
Little children, do not fear,
    He shall not forego His love;
With the banner'd cross unfurl'd,
Fear no tumults of the world.

When He wills, the parting storm
　Shall an azure sky disclose;
Thence shall stoop joy's deathless form
　Smiling on your vanish'd woes;
While the world's brief pleasures flow
To the sea of endless woe.

He who as a Brother died,
　And in the cold grave below
Laid Him by His brethren's side,
　He shall hence before you go,
And take you with Him to dwell
In Godhead unapproachable.

May we here, Lord, die with Thee,
　And with Thy true wisdom wise,
Put on immortality,
　Having treasure in the skies,
Where all things with one accord
Sing the Triune holy Lord.

AT THE MATTINS.

"He shewed Himself alive after His passion by many
infallible proofs, being seen of them forty days, and speaking of the things pertaining to the kingdom of God; and,
being assembled together with them, commanded them
that they should not depart from Jerusalem, but wait for
the promise of the Father."—*Acts* i.

Regnis paternis debitus.

Now hath He oped afar the golden bars
  Of the eternal Heavens, and hath set wide
The skyey gates behind the glittering stars ;—
  Why doth He thus so long on earth abide ?
    'Tis to unfold His kingdom's mysteries,
      In semblances of yore ;
      To shew prophetic eyes
        That look'd before,
  How hidden lay in ancient shadows dim
      The wings of Seraphim,
  All bright-bedropp'd with colours of the
        skies.
  Lo, where the boy up old Moriah's hill,
    The wood upon his shoulders lain,
        Is climbing to be slain,
    Obedient to his father's will :

    Or, in the dark Egyptian land,
    Where the blood marks the lintel high,
    In armèd haste and staff in hand
    Doth ready-harness'd Israel stand,
    And death's dread angel passes by.
        To you, His chosen band,

O pledge of love! to tend and keep
He doth bequeath His scatter'd sheep;
To you to loose and bind is given,
What He shall loose and bind in Heaven.

O Lord, 'tis he who with Thee dies,
  With Thee shall rise above;
May we the things of earth despise,
  The things of Heaven to love.

Praise to the Father, and the Son
  Who bursts death's prison-bars,
Praise to the Spirit, ever One,
  Who leads us to the stars.

St. John in the Island of Patmos.

"I John, who also am your brother, and companion in tribulation, and in the kingdom and patience of Jesus Christ, was in the Isle that is called Patmos, for the word of God and for the testimony of Jesus Christ."—*Rev.* i.

Jussu tyranni pro fide.

John, by a tyrant's stern command,
Is exiled on a sea-girt strand;
But his free spirit takes her flight
Into the regions of the light.

And there his awe-struck soul before
Stands He who lives for evermore,
Who as a lamb gave up His breath,
And as a lion vanquish'd death.

And now before his ravish'd eyes,
He brings His kingdom's mysteries;
The faith sown by His martyrs' blood,
Which through all lands shall spread
    abroad.

O Lord, the power baptismal give
With Thee to die, with Thee to live,
To tread on earthly things, and love
The better things that are above.

All glory and dominion
To God the Father, Spirit, Son,
Who hath broke through our prison-bars,
And leads us to the happy stars.

St. Barnabas the Apostle.

Cælo datur quiescere.

Crown'd with immortal jubilee
  Thy soul this day set free,
To the calm Heavens from earth did pass,
  O holy Barnabas!

He, for whose sake, at whose dear call,
  Thou gavest up thine all:
He shall thine all, thy treasure be,
  Lasting eternally.

'Mid fasting, prayer, and holy hands,
  Lo, 'mid the saints he stands,
The Spirit's high behest to bear,
  Christ's Heaven-sent messenger.

Thou hast with Paul in labours stood,
  Blest bond of brotherhood!
One in the mandate sent from high,
  And one in charity.

To what barbaric shores away
  Did ye that light convey,
When boldly from your race ye turn'd,
  Who Faith's glad message spurn'd?

Lord, when to us, an offer'd guest,
  Shall come that Spirit blest,
Let not our hearts Heaven's bounty slight,
  Deeming their darkness light !

All glory and all praise to Thee
  Thrice holy Trinity,
Who hast disclosed in this our night
  Thine everlasting light !

The Nativity of St. John the Baptist.

AT THE FIRST VESPERS.

"Behold, I will send you Elijah the prophet before the coming of the great and dreadful day of the Lord: and he shall turn the hearts of the fathers to the children, and the hearts of the children to their fathers, lest I come and smite the earth with a curse."—Mal. iv.

Christe, prolapsi reparator orbis.

CHRIST, who dost build the world again,
Cleanse Thou our heart from guilty stain,
That we may speak in holy strain
    The Baptist's festival.
Of mighty prophets he foretold,
Himself a mighty prophet bold,
    Yea, mightier than they all.

E'en now the unborn harbinger
Doth feel the awful Presence near,
Exulting the dread news to bear,
    And spotless Lamb to meet;
And thou who hast in silence hung
Shalt find full soon an unchain'd tongue,
    Thy first-born Child to greet.

Yea, thou thyself, a sudden seer,
Shalt sing to the astonish'd ear
Glad tidings, words of awful fear,
　　And big with mighty things;
And who is He, now Israel cries,
Whose glory thus, like orient skies,
　　Around his cradle springs?

Thee whom Thy creatures all confess
In everlasting blessedness,
Thee, Three in One, Thee, Lord, we bless,
　　Who, ere Thy rise below,
Didst send the holy harbinger
In Thy preparings, like a star,
　　Before the Sun to go.

AT MIDNIGHT.

"The Lord said unto me, Say not, I am a child; for thou shalt go to all that I shall send thee, and whatsoever I command thee thou shalt speak."—*Jer.* i.

Exiit cunis pretiosus infans.

Now from his cradle comes the child,
　　By the Most High
Train'd for His own great ministry:
He, far from man, drinks in the wild,
The springs of wisdom undefiled:

Far 'mid the desert caves profound,
　　'Mid low-brow'd rocks,
Where every noise lorn echo mocks,

The bees that in the rock abound,
And mountain streams, the only sound.

With limbs long-train'd to hardihood,
  The camel's hair
Wrapt rudely round his body bare,
There in the wild Christ's soldier stood,
The desert spoils his only food.

With strong-bent hope his soul doth burn
  From Satan's thrall
That faithless nation to recall,—
That fathers might of children learn,
And children to their fathers turn.

And now to God all praise declare,
  In might arrayed,
The Father who the world hath made,
The Son who doth the world repair,
And Spirit that doth keep it fair.

AT THE MATTINS.

"O Zion, that bringest good tidings, get thee up into
the high mountain; lift up thy voice with strength; lift
it up, be not afraid, say unto the cities of Judah, Behold
your God!"—*Isa.* xl.

Nunc suis tandem novus e latebris.

Lo, from the desert homes,
  Where he hath hid so long,
The new Elias comes,
  In sternest wisdom strong.

The voice that cries
  Of Christ from high,
  And judgment nigh
From opening skies.

Your God e'en now doth stand,
  Within Heaven's opening door,
His fan is in His hand,
  And He will purge His floor;
    The wheat He claims
      And with Him stows,
      The chaff He throws
    To deathless flames.

Ye haughty mountains, bow
  Your sky-aspiring heads;
Ye valleys, hiding low,
  Lift up your gentle meads,
    Make His ways plain
      Your King before:
      For evermore
    He comes to reign.   .

Let Thy dread voice around,
  Thou harbinger of light,
On our dull ears still sound,
  Lest here we sleep in night,
    Till judgment come,
      And on our path
      Shall burst the wrath,
    And deathless doom.

O God, with love's sweet might,
Who dost anoint and arm
Christ's soldier for the fight
With spells that shield from harm,
Thrice blessèd Three,
Heaven's endless days
Shall sing Thy praise
Eternally.

AT THE SECOND VESPERS.

"This is he of whom it is written, Behold, I send My messenger before Thy face, which shall prepare Thy way before Thee."—*Matt.* xi.

Quid moras nectis ?   Domino jubenti.

WHY linger'st thou, great John! thy Lord commands;
Yea, He who washes souls with living fires
More pure than liquid lightnings, He requires
And bears the cleansing river from thy hands.

How sunk thy soul, when there in Jordan's bed
He bow'd His head, before thee all unmeet
To take the sandals from His sacred feet,
Before thee bow'd His more than holy head !

See from the heavens, descending like a dove,
There hovers now a brightly-glowing cloud ;
The unutterable voice is heard aloud,
The awful Three in One, below, above.

But thou art bent to preach the avenging rod
  Of justice, and, the flag of peace unfurl'd,
  The victim come to cleanse the guilty world,—
To point out the unspotted Lamb of God.

Careless of thine own honour, thou to cease
  Didst hasten, like the star before the day,
  Willing thyself to vanish hence away,—
'Tis meet that thou depart, and He increase.

But not alone shalt thou with thy life's breath
  Bear witness,—one thing yet to thee remains,
  Boldly the truth to speak, and bear the
      chains,
And go before thy Lord in murderous death.

In Thee our strains shall end, Thee ever sing,
  The eternal Father, and the eternal Son,
  And the eternal Spirit, Three in One,
Whom Heaven and earth adore, sole God and
      King.

St. Paul.

"I, brethren, when I came to you, came not with excellency of speech or of wisdom; for I determined not to know any thing among you, but Jesus Christ, and Him crucified."—1 Cor. ii.

Enough, O Paul, enough, and now
A crown in Heaven awaits thy brow,
Thy earthly toils are nearly done,
Thy heavenly prize is all but won;
Long toss'd by ills on land and sea,
The shore is all but gain'd by thee.

Long time 'mid stonings, rods, and chains,
Watchings and cares and dying pains,
Thee Christ upon His cross doth hold,
In daily dyings now grown old;
He bids thee now no more remain,
And unto thee to die is gain.

Love's tender bowels yearning strong,—
They for whom thou didst toil so long
In travailings of second birth,—
Thy children hold thee still to earth:
The time for thy release is come,
And ready is thy heavenly home.

When 'mid the Twelve thy throne is set,
And we shall be for judgment met,
May we whom from the dead of night
God calls in thee to see His light,
For ever with the angelic host
Sing Father, Son, and Holy Ghost.

AT THE MATTINS.

"Yes, doubtless, and I count all things but loss for the excellency of the knowledge of Christ Jesus my Lord; that I may know Him, and the fellowship of His sufferings, being made conformable unto His death."—*Philipp.* iii.

Sudore sat two fides.

Yes, thou hast drain'd thy Master's cup,
  His bitter woes ador'd,
And by thy sufferings hast fill'd up
  The suffering of thy Lord.

Not only on thy body borne
  Thy Master's mark impress'd,
But He within thy spirit worn
  Himself doth manifest.

So, holy Paul, thou liv'st no more,
  Art dead with Him that died;
But in thy bosom evermore
  Doth live the Crucified.

Then rise aloof, and the third heaven,
　Once heard, shall now to Thee,
From out its inmost fountains given,
　Break everlastingly.

O in thy teaching, while we may,
　Still let us more abide,
And follow thee on Christ's blest way,
　The follower and the guide.

Grant this, O Thou in Spirit one,
　Thrice holy, One and Three,
And ever be to Thee alone,
　All glory be to Thee.

The blessed Virgin Mary visiting Elisabeth.

" How beautiful upon the mountains are the feet of
one that bringeth good tidings."—Isa. lii.

Montes, superbum verticem.

Ye mountains, bend ye low,
  O'er which the Virgin flies,
  To whom the starry skies
Would their glad summits bow.

In maiden fear conceal'd,
  Long hid in quiet home,
  She now abroad doth come,
With charity her shield.

She flies without delay,—
  She flies from human eyes,—
  Not to be seen, she flies,
And fears lest aught betray.

Blest earth, whereon she trod,
  Put forth your fragrance sweet;—
  Blest hills, that felt her feet,
The mother with her God.

More blest ye friends, whose guest
She now doth silence break,
Of heavenly things to speak,
And where her footsteps rest.

The Father, who doth send,
The Son, who saves the lost,
The guiding Holy Ghost,
We praise Thee without end.

St. Mary Magdalene.

AT THE FIRST VESPERS.

"What a word is this! for with authority and power
He commandeth the unclean spirits, and they come out."
—*Luke* iv. 36.

Procul maligni cedite spiritus.

AVAUNT, ye fiends unclean,
    It is our God commands;
Spare the worn Magdalene
    From your tormenting bands:
They hear Christ's voice in dread dismay—
The seven-fold fiends are fled away.

Now, to herself restor'd,
    She follows Christ alone,
And treasures every word
    Which she from Him hath won;—
And now, beneath the accursèd wood
Whereon He hung, she weeping stood.

She, haply, fondly deems
    That she would bear His pains,
The weight she little dreams
    Of all our guilty stains;—
His dying head she sees Him bow,
And silence speaks her solemn woe.

To Father, and to Son,
  As hath been aye of yore;
To Spirit, ever one,
  Be praise for evermore:
In whom our souls, all newly born,
Kindle with fires of heavenly morn.

———

AT MIDNIGHT.

"They shall look upon Me, and they shall mourn as
one mourneth for his only son, and shall be in bitterness
for Him, as one that is in bitterness for his first-born."
—Zech. xii.

Plagis Magistri saucia.

SAD Mary feels in her own breast
  Her Master's bleeding wounds;
Love stronger burns by griefs opprest,
  And now with tears abounds.

No raging crowds her spirit meek,
  No deeds of blood appal;
'Mid soldiers fierce she dares to seek
  A hated criminal.

Ah, Mary, thou dost little know
  What good doth thee surround;
Seeking the dead, while death e'en now
  Receives his mortal wound.

He whom thou lovest thee shall claim,
  Arous'd from death's cold sleep;
Thee first He calls, thee by thy name,
  And bids thee not to weep.

O might I touch Thy sacred feet,
  Adoring, cling to Thee!
Nay, raise thy thoughts to joys more
    meet,
  For immortality.

The promises are fully wrought,
  First of Apostles thou,
Sent to Apostles, by thee taught
  The tidings glad to know.

All love and glory be to Thee,
  The Father, Spirit, Son;
Coequal, coeternal Three,
  Thrice blessèd, Holy One.

AT THE MATTINS.

"I love them that love Me, and those that seek Me
early shall find Me."—*Prov. viii.*

Maria sacro saucia vulnere.

WHY for thy Lord dost thou thus weep and
    mourn,
Like one half-broken-hearted and forlorn?
No need for Him that thou shouldst mourn

He, whom thou seekest in the murky tomb,
Hath sprung bright and victorious from the
        gloom ;
He lives, He greatly lives for evermore ;
See wide the rocks ope the sepulchral door.

Why bring'st thou myrrh and spices, offerings
        meet
For livid corpses in their winding sheet ?
His body blooms with immortality,
Meet to return to His paternal sky.

Thy tears proclaim the greatness of thy love,
Nor doth thy Lord thy flowing tears reprove ;
Hear'st thou ! and know'st thou not that voice
        adored ?
'Tis thine own name ! He speaks—thy God and
        Lord.

Now go, first witness and first messenger,
Throughout the city thy glad tidings bear,
And teach the Twelve that Christ Himself is
        nigh,
And, wheresoe'er thou speakest, standing by.

All love, and praise, and majesty be Thine,
Father, and Son, and Holy Spirit Divine ;
Quicken'd by whom our bodies shall return,
And in immortal bloom for ever burn.

St. Peter in Prison.

AT THE VESPERS.

"I have made thee this day a defenced city, and an iron pillar, and brazen walls against the whole land, against the kings of Judah, against the princes thereof, against the priests thereof, and against the people of the land. And they shall fight against thee: but they shall not prevail against thee; for I am with thee, saith the Lord, to deliver thee."—*Jer.* I.

Qui Christiano gloriantur nomine.

No brazen fetters have the captive bound,
Who glories in the Name invincible;
   Nor the dread sound
Of sentry watching by the bolted cell;
He in his chains hath truer freedom found.

'Mid purer heavens his unchain'd spirit doth
     stray,
The ponderous iron is by love made light,
   And the clear ray
Breaks in the prison-house of gloomy night
From the bright courts of ever-during day.

Blest chains, that prove no guilty criminal,
But one train'd in Christ's school, serenely bent
   To suffer all,—

To Him all praise, all power, all majesty,
The Holy Son, who for His people died,
    All glory be,—
All glory be to Christ the Crucified,
All glory to the Holy One and Three.

AT THE MATTINS.

"Wisdom forsook not the righteous, but delivered him
from sinners; she went down with him into the pit, and
left him not in bonds."—*Wisdom* x.

Petrum, tyranne, quid catenis obruis.

Where the prison bars surround him,
  In his chains shall Peter dwell;
Where the sentinel hath bound him,
  Pacing by his gloomy cell?
    What shall avail
Prison, chains, or sentinel?

Lo, a light, from Heaven descending,
  Glimmers, like a beauteous star,
An Angel o'er the Saint is bending,
  And the wing'd night is fled afar.
    His chains are burst,
Open is the massy bar.

Where the heavenly guide is leading,
  Peter follows, firm and bold;
All as in a dream proceeding
  Through the portals dark and cold;
    And now, amazed,
Doth the Almighty's hand behold.

ST. PETER IN PRISON.

We in prison-chains are sleeping,
  Chains of sin which Angels see;
Dunnest night our soul is steeping—
  Christ, our light, our liberty,
    Break Thou our chains,
  Lighten us, and make us free.

Highest praise to Thee, the Highest,
  Infinite, dread Trinity;
Who, awhile our spirits triest,
  Fitting them to dwell with Thee,
    Thee adoring,
  Everlasting, Holy Three.

The Transfiguration.

AT THE FIRST AND SECOND VESPERS.

"The sun shall be ashamed when the Lord of hosts shall
reign in Mount Zion, and before His ancients gloriously."
—Isa. xxiv.

Hoc jussa quondam rumpimus.

Bring, happy day, to light
Things which dark-mantling Night
   In envious silence hath so long been stealing;
When, on the mountain floor,
Before the three of yore,
   The Son of man His glory was revealing:
And, through His flesh's shrouding shrine,
Illuminating ran the effluence Divine.

The full irradiance flows,
To every limb it goes,
   With snowy light His fiery garments
      blending;
Now awe-struck silence quakes,
And the live thunder speaks,
   From the bright cloud in majesty descending;
There sounds the unutterable Voice,
  Proclaiming His dear Son, the everlasting
      choice.

With low-brow'd awe profound,
Be silent on the ground,
  The Lord of all is in His holy hill ;
And now, with voice of fear,
Let angel hosts draw near,
  While all the listening world is still,
To sing the Spirit and the Word,
And Father, whose dread voice was in
    the thunder heard.

AT MIDNIGHT.

"O Lord my God, Thou art become exceeding glorious,
Thou art clothed with majesty and honour. Thou deckest
Thyself with light as it were with a garment."—Psalm civ.

Quam nos potenter allicis.

How strongly and how sweetly still
Thou, Christ, dost draw the human will,
      And gently prove,
Whether Thou dost Thyself reveal,
Or from our senses dost conceal,
      'Tis both in love.

The Father calls, and for Thy sake
Shall us too for His children take ;
      And, through Heaven's door,
The glory which doth break on Thee
Are rays of immortality
      That go before.

What saith the Father, speaking loud?
And what the Son beneath the cloud?
          Now all are gone,
The shadows fleet, around again
Silence keeps watch, there doth remain
          The truth alone.

Again Thou dost Thy form resume,
A Victim ready for the tomb,
          And thence descend
In lowliness ineffable,
Thy Father's mandate to fulfil,
          Unto the end.

O Christ, who now Thyself dost hide,
May faith our darkling spirits guide,
          And firmly hold,
That when these fleshly vessels break,
We of Thy goodness may partake,
          And Thee behold.

And with an undefiled tongue
May sing the Spirit, ever young,
          Through Heaven's long days,
Sing Thee, whose voice was heard aloud,
Sing Thee, who wast beneath the cloud,
          In endless praise.

AT THE MATTINS.

Jesu dulcedo cordium.

Jesu, the heart's own sweetness, and true light,
    Thou art the secret Fountain that o'erflows
The weary soul, surpassing all delight,
    In whom each anxious longing finds repose.

Stay with us, Lord, and with Thy kindly ray
    Enlighten our dark spirits, at whose birth
Dark shades shall flee the opening eye of day,
    And sweetness shall revive the drooping
        earth.

When Thou the heart dost visit, all things seem
    Made new, Truth shines in her unclouded
        form,
Emerging from the world as from a dream;
    And Love, her face beholding, waxeth warm.

Good Jesus, while time's scroll I still unfold,
    Do Thou to me Thy love make manifest,
That I, 'mid clouds that wrap me, may behold
    Thine everlasting glory, and find rest.

He whom Thy love makes glad as with new
        wine,
  He knows that knowledge which is from
        above;
Full blest is he; that fulness is Divine,
  And there is nothing else that he can love,

Thou art the Fount of pity; as it flows
  All drink of Thine abundance infinite:
Thou art the only Sun Thy country knows;
  Scatter the clouds, and shew us Thy true
        light.

St. John the Baptist beheaded in Prison.

AT THE FIRST VESPERS.

"I will speak of Thy testimonies also even before kings, and will not be ashamed."—Psalm cxix.

Quis ille sylvis e penetralibus.

Who hither comes from shrines of the dark
  wood,
 With voice that sternly cries; and as he
  goes
Hang on his words a growing multitude !
 His is no brow that swells with fancied woes,
 Nurs'd in a palace or a court's repose :
No reed is he which to the moaning gale
Waves its tall shadow in the moonlight pale.

For thrice-ten years in desert haunts profound
 He hath been rear'd to holy hardihood,
And the deep wild now hears again the sound
 Of her Elijah in the solitude ;
 Who with his spirit bold and might endued
The thunders of God's law proclaims aloud,
To soldier, Pharisee, and humble crowd.

And now admitted to the kingly hall
    Unto the subtle tyrant he draws near ;
No coward fears the Prophet's heart appal,
    No courtly favour wins, nor listening ear
    His holy admonitions *glad to hear ;*
But e'en in kingly ears, severe and free,
He warning speaks of foul adultery.

To Thee, O God, the Father, Spirit, Son,
    To Thee, O holy, holy, holy Three,
To Thee, O blessèd Three, O awful One,
    O Thou who dwellest in eternity,
    All love, all might, all glory be to Thee,
A sacrifice to Thee our hearts we raise,
Make Thou them meet to sing Thine endless
        praise.

AT MIDNIGHT.

"I am horribly afraid for the ungodly that forsake
Thy law."—Psalm cxix.

Impune vati non erit, impotens.

Non shall the Prophet 'scape unharm'd ;
The adultress, stung with guilt, with fury
        arm'd,
    Fires the fierce king : ever allied
Murder and lust shall ravin side by side.
    Alas where guilty passion reigns!
Innocent hands are given to felon chains,
    But that free voice which truth commands
Cannot be held with chains, nor feel the prison
        bands.

E'en in the dungeon's silent gloom
He has a herald voice as from the tomb;
　And bids his orphan children go
That they the Lord of life by proof may know.
　The axe of death prepared to meet,
The prisoner triumphs in his dungeon seat:
　The tyrant trembles, consoious sin
Keeps watch with silent scourge, and sleepless
　　　eye within.

O Lord, our hearts and hands we raise,
A sacrifice to Thee of endless praise,
　Who dwellest in the infinite
Of unapproachable and blessèd light;
　Where the Seraphic hosts do cry,
Holy, holy, holy, God Almighty,—
　The Father, Spirit, and the Son,
The inconceivèd Three, the unutterable Onė.

AT THE MATTINS.

"I say unto you that Elias is come already, and they
knew him not, but have done unto him whatsoever they
listed."—*Matt.* xvii.

Ecce, saltantis pretium puellæ.

BEHOLD, the price of courtly dance,
　The fruit of the forbidden glance,
　　The head of Christ's great harbinger!
　The voice, which did repentance call,
　From sylvans rude to palace hall;
Hush'd is that voice and tongue, and ne'er
　　again shall stir.

Lazarus, Mary, and Martha visited by Christ.

AT THE FIRST VESPERS.

"If a man love Me he will keep My words; and My
Father will love him, and We will come unto him, and
make Our abode with him."—John xiv.

Flagrans amore, perditos.

As Jesus sought His wandering sheep,
  With weary toil opprest,
He came to Martha's lowly roof,
  A lov'd and honour'd Guest.

Blessèd art Thou, whose threshold poor
  Those holy feet have trod,
To wait on so Divine a Guest,
  And to receive thy God!

While Martha serves with busy feet,
  In reverential mood
Meek Mary sits beside the Judge,
  And feeds on heavenly food.

Yea, Martha soon herself shall sit
  The eternal word to hear,
And shall forget the festal board,
  To feast on holier cheer.

Sole rest of all who come to Thee,
  O'er all our works preside,
That we may have in Thee, at last,
  The part that shall abide.   Amen.

AT MIDNIGHT.

"The Lord your God proveth you, to know whether ye
love the Lord your God with all your heart and with all
your soul."—*Deut.* xiii.

Redditum luci, Domino vocante.

Sing the Redeemer's saving might!
The crowd aghast at the dread sight,
A buried man burst forth to light,
      Again to run
Our weary round of day and night,
      And see the sun!

He whose blest roof to Christ supplies
Shelter and kindly ministries,
Deep in the rock he buried lies—
      Buried and gone!
Corruption's prey, hid from our eyes
      In the cold stone.

Worship, and love, and faltering fear,
And hope awake—Hadst Thou been here,
We had not mourned a brother's bier;
      And well we know
Whate'er Thou askest God will hear—
      Yea, even now.

Lord, art Thou weeping for Thy friend,
Whom death again to life shall lend?
Or doth it not in pity rend
      Thy heart in twain
To think so many have an end,
      Nor rise again?

Triune Jehovah, Thee we crave,
When we shall lay us in the grave,
From second death Thy people save;
      Our spirits still
With Thy Baptismal virtue lave,
      And keep from ill.

AT THE MATTINS.

"Thus saith the Lord God, Behold, I will open your graves, and cause you to come up out of your graves. And ye shall know that I am the Lord."—*Ezekiel* xxxvii.

Panditur saxo tumulus remoto.

OPEN is the rocky tomb
And a voice is in the gloom;
And a sound is on the ear;
And the dead that sound doth hear!
For God Himself is near.

Amazing sight! the spirit now
Hath his former seat I trow;
For the dead doth stretch his hands
Through his swaddling bands,
Darkly groping for his way,
In the light of living day.

Now forth he stands
    With a stare,
Survivor of himself and heir.
His bands about him broken lie,
And away old Death doth fly,
Glad to resign his victory.
O Lord, this earnest of thy sway
Gives prelude of the judgment day.
    Thee we pray,
When we shall resign our breath,
Save us from the second death ;
From the second death us save !
So may we, rising from the wintry grave,
    Through everlasting spring,
The Father, Son, and Spirit sing.

                      Amen.

AT THE SECOND VESPERS.

"Come, ye blessed of My Father, inherit the kingdom prepared for you; for I was an hungred, and ye gave Me meat: I was thirsty, and ye gave Me drink: I was a stranger, and ye took Me in."—*Matt.* xxv.

Intrante Christo Bethanicam domum.

Lo, Christ hath gone to Bethany,
And Simon hath prepar'd the board ;
Amid that blessèd company,
There let us stand, and see the Lord.

What doth the busy Martha seek?
Is that the dead doth sit and eat?
But where is Mary—she so meek?
She leaneth o'er her Saviour's feet.

Hanging her locks, in holy fear,
She opes the odorous 'nard, 'tis she
O'er His blest head, and far and near,
'Tis fragrant with her piety.

Oh, let not whispering envy blame,
Nor avarice in wisdom's guise,
The anointing of the dying Lamb,
For His approaching obsequies.

Where o'er the earth, from clime to clime,
The messenger of peace shall call,
So far shall bear recording time
Meek Mary's blest memorial.

Then may we praise Him without blame
The Father, Son, and Spirit's Name,
The Son who came meek Mary's Guest,
Who now in Him hath endless rest.

The Blessed Virgin Mary.

Mortale, cælo tolle, genus, caput.

MORTAL race, enwrapt in gloom
Of thine awe-inspiring doom,
Lift thy head above the tomb.

Night's black horrors troop away,
And a white emerging ray
Speaks the coming of the day.

Now earth's teeming breast portends,
And high Heaven to meet it bends,
And the big rain-drop descends.

Lo, from Jesse's root this hour,
Springs a shoot touch'd by the shower,
And reveals a nascent flower.

Heaven's own dews shall on Him rest,
Keep His stainless leaflets blest,
And embalm His opening breast.

Faith, chaste Fear, and holy Love,
And strict Justice from above,
All around His coming move.

Ancient Time, from days of yore,
Eagerly hath bent before,
And hath watch'd the opening door.

Haste thou on, approaching morn,
And Thou, glorious Child be born,
Only hope of earth forlorn.

Praise the Triune God of all,
Who in pity for our thrall,
Doth unto His mercy call.

St. Michael and All Angels.

AT THE FIRST VESPERS.

" His throne was like the fiery flame; thousand thousands
ministered unto Him, and ten thousand times ten thousand
stood before Him."—*Dan.* vii.

Christe qui sedes Olympo.

O CHRIST, who sitt'st with God on high,
  In equal majesty,
Where angels in Thy glory's blaze
  Do tremble as they gaze ;
Grant us unblamed to speak in song
  Of that celestial throng.

One o'er the rest with shining sheen,
  · And glittering sword is seen ;
'Tis he who crush'd the dragon's might
  In the victorious fight,
And hurl'd him in black overthrow,
  Unto the deeps below.

With lifted arm, and thund'ring cry,
  " Who shall our God defy ?"
Thou stood'st; then the dark rebel rout
  Fell scatter'd all about ;
And He who gave the victory,
  Gave thee the crown on high.

O fairest in that wingèd band,
  Where the bright heralds stand;
To Thee the highest place is given
  Within the courts of Heaven,
To ope and close the starry door,
  And bring the Judge before.

'Tis thine to set the spirit free
  In death's last agony,
Coming in calm unearthly light,
  To walk through death's dim night,
And bear her from her chains away,
  To mansions of the day.

Glory to the Eternal Three,
  Equal in majesty;
To Him who did our being give,
  Who died that we might live,
Whose breath Divine doth us restore,
  And cherish evermore.   Amen.

AT THE MATTINS.

"Blessed art Thou upon the throne of Thy kingdom, and
to be praised and glorified above all for ever. Blessed art
Thou that beholdest the depths, and sittest upon the
cherubims."—Dan. iii.

Mille quem stipant solio sedentem.

O Thou, around whose everlasting throne
Throng countless hosts, a glorious multitude,
Free from all bodily weight; make us Thine
    own,
Whom Thou to Thee hast hallow'd with Thy
    blood.

Those happy seats, wherein Thy kingdom lies,
Beyond the stars, for us Thou dost prepare,
And ever from those sweet societies
Thou sendest friendly guides to lead us there.

May the repeller of unearthly harms,
Great Michael, champion of the law divine,
Ever be o'er us with ethereal arms
To shield us from the foe, and keep us Thine !

May Gabriel his sweet aid around us plant,
And in the might of God's own fortitude
Come oft from Heaven, a glorious pursuivant,
To visit us with messages of good.

May Raphael's gentle art and healing hand,
Which gave blind Tobit old to see the light,
Wave all around his soothing influence bland,
Scattering our body's ills, and spirit's blight.

From Thee, sole Fountain of all good below,
King of the heavenly hosts, our praise begun,
In Thee shall end. 'Tis truth Thy name to
        know,
And life to trust in Thee, the Three in One.
                              Amen.

Guardian Angels.

AT THE VESPERS.

"Are they not all ministering spirits, sent forth to minister for them who shall be heirs of salvation?"—*Heb.* i.

Custodes hominum psallimus Angelos.

AND are there then celestial habitants,
Whom a kind Father's care around us plant,
Sent to walk with us in our earthly trance?

Yes, Heaven's undying outcast, in dark hate
Of those whom God hath call'd to his lost
    state,
Ever around our pathway lies in wait.

And these blest guardians at high Heaven's
    command
Dwell round about our homes, with unseen
    wand
Watchful to ward his wiles, and hold our
    hand.

All praise to God the Father of the Word,
All praise to God the Son with one accord,
All praise to Thee, the Holy Ghost ador'd.

AT THE MATTINS.

"I say unto you, that in Heaven their angels do always behold the face of My Father, which is in heaven."
Matt. xviii.

Regnator orbis summus et arbiter.

WHERE the angelic hosts adore Thee,
   Thou o'er earth and Heaven dost reign,
At Thy word they rose before Thee,
   And Thy breath doth them sustain.
From high angels Thee attending,
   Thou dost faithful guardians send ;
In mysterious ways descending,
   May they keep us to the end.

Keep us, else with wiles deceiving
   The persuader of all ill,
Round his deadly meshes weaving,
   The lost soul will rend and kill.
All Creation bows before Thee,
   Father, Son, and Holy Ghost:
Highest angels that adore Thee
   Succour and sustain the lost.

On the Vigil of All Saints' Day.

AT MIDNIGHT.

"God shall wipe away all tears from their eyes ; and there shall be no more death, neither sorrow, nor crying, neither shall there be any more pain."—*Rev. xxi.*

Pugnate Christi milites.

SOLDIERS, who to Christ belong,
In your burnish'd faith be strong,
For God's promise it is sure,
His rewards they shall endure.

    Come away
Where no shadows in a glass,
Where no things that come and pass
    To decay—
But the leaf that shall not fade,
And the lights that know no shade
    Ever stay.

Where, the happy skies above,
Is the house of them that love
    All the day ;
And good spirits o'er our head,
As on happy stars they tread,
    Sing alway.

Here on earth ye can ßat clasp
Things that perish in the grasp.
    While ye may,
Lift your faces to the skies,
God Himself shall be your prize.
    Come away

Where the happy heavenly host
Sing Father, Son, and Holy Ghost;
For His promise it is sure,
His rewards they shall endure.

AT THE MATTINS.

"And there shall be no more night there; and they need
no candle, neither light of the sun; for the Lord God giveth
them light."—*Rev.* xxii.

Cælestis O Jerusalem.

O HEAVENLY Jerusalem
  Of everlasting halls,
Thrice blessèd are the people
  Thou storest in thy walls!

Thou art the golden mansion,
  Where Saints for ever sing;
The seat of God's own chosen,
  The palace of the King.

There God for ever sitteth,
  Himself of all the crown;
The Lamb the light that shineth,
  And never goeth down.

Nought to that seat approacheth
  Their sweet peace to molest;
They sing their God for ever,
  Nor day nor night they rest.

Calm Hope from thence is leaning,
  To her our longings bend;
No short-lived toil shall daunt us
  For joys that cannot end.

To Christ the Sun that lightens
  His Church, above, below;
To Father and to Spirit
  All things created bow.

All Saints' Day.

AT THE FIRST AND SECOND VESPERS.

"Thou wast slain, and hast redeemed us to God by Thy
blood out of every kindred, and tongue, and people, and
nation; and hast made us unto our God kings and priests."
Rev. v.

Cælo quos eadem gloria consecrat.

Ye that are now in heavenly glory one
May we together join, with earthly voice,
Hymning your everlasting victories, won
By arduous labours and the better choice.

Now love and unveil'd truth doth feed for aye,
And ye drink full of joy's o'erflowing wells,
Where slakes the soul her thirst that cannot
    die,
And by the sacred fountain ever dwells.

From inmost shrines from whence the God-
    head streams,
The King Himself, with His own countenance,
Shines o'er you, and unsparing of His beams,
Fills the soul's dwelling with His radiance.

From out the golden altar, 'neath the throne,
Blood of the Innocent for mercy pleads;
He offer'd once to Him that sits thereon,

'Mid lightnings numberless, thro' the dim
    vast
Of light, the adoring elders bow them down,
To Him whose kingdom shall for ever last ;
And each before Him casts his golden crown.

Nations and languages of countless tongue,
With jub'lant palm, and robes wash'd white
   in blood,
For ever sing the inexpressive song —
Him the Thrice Holy and the Only Good.

Glory on earth, and glory be above,
To Father, Son, and Spirit ever blest,
Who with the just dispensings of their love
All to their fulness fill with perfect rest.

AT THE COMPLINE.

"Ye are come unto Mount Sion, and unto the city of the
living God, the heavenly Jerusalem, and to an innumerable
company of Angels, to the general assembly and church of
the first-born, which are written in Heaven, and to God the
Judge of all, and to the spirits of just men made perfect,
and to Jesus the Mediator of the New Covenant."—*Heb.* xii.

Vos sancti proceres, vos superum chori.

Ye saintly choirs, that round the regal seat,
Through Heaven's eternal palace, endless
    throng,
May we with voice for mortal not unmeet,
   Join your eternal song.

Myriads of spiritual hosts the throne around
Stand with their votive offerings, day and
    night;
There doth the herald Baptist dive profound
    In the deep flood of light.

There they, whose voice sounding Christ cru-
    cified,
Like thunder went about from strand to strand,
With the anointed Prophets by their side,
    The twelve great Preachers stand.

There in their purple stole are Martyrs seen,
And Virgins white that knew no earthly flame,
Like roses which with lilies blend between,
    The victim's wreath to frame.

They who have fed their flocks are feeding
    there
In God's own fulness, brought for ever near;
And they who wept,—a Father's calming care
    Wipes away every tear.

Glory to Him from whom all blessings flow,
To Him who ransom'd man's lost destinies,
To Him who kindles in the soul below
    The torch that never dies !

AT THE MATTINS.

"White robes were given unto every one of them; and
it was said unto them, that they should rest yet for a little
season, until their fellow-servants also, and their brethren
should be fulfilled."—Rev. vi.

Hymnis dum resonat curia cælitum.

Ye in the house of heavenly morn
Attune your golden hymns for ever;
While we beside Time's lovely river
　　Have hung our tuneless harps forlorn,
　　And, exiled from our country, mourn.

When shall the soul put forth her flight,
Escapèd from her earthly prison,
'Mid your glad choirs in glory risen,
　　See Truth in her own fountain bright,
　　And have her dwelling in the light?

From her the mists shall then be gone,
When, without cloud and without motion,
She stands beside the crystal ocean,
　　Which is before the Eternal's throne;
　　And we shall know as we are known.

Safe in your heavenly haven, ye
Behold us on the stormy billow,
Nought but the rude wave for our pillow.
  Christ, lead us to that port to Thee,
  Thou Star that light'st eternity.

To Him from whom all blessings flow,
To Father, Son, in earth, in Heaven,
And unto Him be glory given,
  Who doth with light the spirit sow,
  And kindle heavenly seed below.

The Octave of All Saints.

(ON THE MORTAL REMAINS OF THE DEAD.)

AT THE VESPERS.

"If the Spirit of Him that raised up Jesus from the dead
dwell in you, He that raised up Christ from the dead shall
also quicken your mortal bodies by His Spirit that dwelleth
in you."—*Romans* viii.

O vos unanimes Christianum chori.

REVERENCE their poor and sadly dear remains!
  Folded in peace their earthly vesture lies,
  Dear pledges, left below, but thence to rise,
Pledges of heavenly bodies, free from pains!
And here ye may lift up your thankful strains,
  Ye Christian companies.   The spirit flies,
  And hath its recompence in quiet skies,
And leaves with you below its broken chains :
  Yet for their bones meek Piety shall plead,
  Blest Piety, which honoureth the dead!
Though scatter'd far and wide, yet God's own eye
  Doth keep them that they perish not; and when
  The promised hour shall come, their God again

His habitation, each there, moulded by His
    grace,
Shall live and find a sure abiding-place.

To us the places where your ashes lie
    Shall be as altars, whence shall steadier rise
    Our prayers to Heaven ; and that blest Sacfi-
        fice,
Where God the Victim cometh down from high,
Shall consecrate to holier mystery ;
    He here accepts your deaths as join'd with
        His,
    Here builds all in one body, and supplies
Our dying frames with immortality.
    And hence your graves become a tower of aid,
    A refuge from bad thoughts, a sacred shade ;
Until, fresh clad with new and wondrous
        dowers,
    Our flesh shall join th' angelic choirs, and be
A living temple crown'd with heavenly towers ;
    Where evermore the praises shall ascend
    Of the great undivided One and Three,
    And God be all in all, world without end.

AT THE MATTINS.

"Ye are dead, and your life is hid with Christ in God ;
when Christ, who is our life, shall appear, then shall ye
also appear with Him in glory."—*Colos. iii.*

Adeste, sancti, plurimo.

Ye holy ones departed be around ;
Like incense are your memories ; do ye not
   Hear our poor prayers ascend,
   And, hearing them, rejoice !

Your dear remains have moulder'd to their
      dust,
Long since committed to the sorrowing grave !
   But from behind the veil
   Your presence breathes around.

Your hallowing and soothing influence
Fills all our temples, softening our rude hearts ;
   While ye are in new worlds,
   To higher service bound.

Your ashes, which beneath our altars lie,
Breathe a deep spell, divinely eloquent,
   To heal the heart-sick soul,
   And bid bad spirits flee.

To Father, Son, and Spirit, Three in One,
Our Maker, Guide, and Saviour, One in
      Three,
   All praise, all glory be,
   Lasting eternally.

COMMEMORATION OF SAINTS.

Commemoration of Apostles.

AT MIDNIGHT.

"Who maketh the clouds His chariot: and walketh upon
the wings of the wind: He maketh His angels spirits; and
His ministers a flaming fire."—*Psalm civ.*

Supreme, quales, Arbiter.

DISPOSER Supreme,
    And Judge of the earth,
Who choosest for Thine
    The weak and the poor;
To frail earthen vessels,
    And things of no worth,
Entrusting Thy riches
    Which aye shall endure.

Those vessels soon fail,
    Though full of Thy light;
They at Thy decree
    Are broken and gone;
Then brightly appeareth
    The arm of Thy might,
As through the clouds breaking
    The lightnings have shone.

Like clouds are they borne
    To do Thy great will,
And swift as the winds
    About the world go:
All full of Thy Godhead,
    While earth lieth still,
They thunder, they lighten,
    The waters o'erflow.

They thunder—their sound
    It is Christ the Lord!
Then Satan doth fear,
    His citadels fall,
As when the dread trumpets
    Went forth at Thy word,
And on the ground lieth
    The Canaanites' wall.

Ó loud be Thy trump,
    And stirring the sound,
To rouse us, O Lord,
    From sin's deadly sleep;
May lights which Thou kindlest
    In darkness around,
The dull soul awaken
    Her vigils to keep!

All glory to Thee,
    Who art hid from sight,
Yet fillest with love
    The vast infinite;

And reveal'd to our aid
  As One and yet Three,
Dost call us from afar
  Thy glory to see.

AT THE MATTINS.

"O worship the Lord in the beauty of holiness; let the whole earth stand in awe of Him. Tell it out among the heathen that the Lord is King."—*Psalm xcvi.*

Cœlestis aulæ Principes.

Ye captains of a heavenly host,
  Ye princes of a heavenly hall,
Stars of the world, in darkness lost,
  And judges at its funeral.

Lights rising o'er a wintry night,
  With tidings of eternal youth,
On error's long bewilder'd sight
  Emerging with the lamp of truth.

Captains,—but not of spear and shield,
  No rebel hosts with steel to tame,
No arms of eloquence to wield,
  Nought but the lowly Cross of shame.

The chain is riven, and broke the rod,
  The world's long stern captivity,
And we are free to serve our God,
  Whose yoke alone is liberty.

To distant lands His heralds fleet,
  By God's mysterious presence led ;
How beauteous are their passing feet,
  Like morn upon the mountains spread!

To Father, Son, and Holy Ghost
  All glory be as was of old,
Who calleth us in darkness lost
  His saving glory to behold.

AT THE SECOND VESPERS.

"He that now goeth on his way weeping, and beareth
forth good seed, shall doubtless come again with joy, and
bring his sheaves with him."—*Psalm* cxxvi.

Quem misit in terras Deus.

He whom the Father sent to die,
Hath given you His commission high,
The channels of His grace to be,
And vessels of His charity.

The Lamb, which by the wolves was slain,
Sends you as lambs to wolves again ;
They have aside their nature laid,
And lambs by you of wolves are made.

The earth look'd to the offended skies
Teeming with impious sacrifice ;
Now by your sweat 'tis newly dyed,
And by your blood is purified.

New fruits her genial face renew,
Blest by that fertilizing dew ;
How rich the harvest of His grace !
And we in that have found a place.

If Thou who dost the increase give,
Wilt look on us, then we shall live,
Ripen, and grow, and evermore
Be gather'd to Thy heavenly store.

Glory to God, both Three and One,
The Father, Spirit, and the Son,
Who calleth us from dead of night
To see His countenance of light.

Commemoration of Evangelists.

AT THE VESPERS.

"Behold upon the mountains the feet of him, that bringeth good tidings, that publisheth peace."—*Nahum* i.

Christi perennes nuntii.

CHRIST's everlasting messengers,
  Who, from the opening skies,
Traverse the earth in showers of light,
  And sow with mysteries.

The things discern'd by seers of old,
  Behind the shadowy screen,
In the full day have ye beheld,
  With not a veil between.

The things which God as man hath borne,
  Which man as God hath done,
Ye write, as God dictates, to all
  Who see the circling sun.

Though far in space and time apart,
  One Spirit sways you all;
And we in those blest characters
  Hear now that living call.

Glory to God, the Three in One,
  All glory be to Thee,
Who from our darkness callest us
  Thy glorious light to see.

AT THE MATTINS.

"Out of Sion hath God appeared in perfect beauty. Our
God shall come and shall not keep silence."—*Psalm* l.

Sinæ sub alto vertice.

WHEN from the mount the Law was given
  Sinai with terrors rang;
Thunderings, and darkness lightning-riven,
  And the loud trumpet's clang,
Confess'd our present God come down from
    Heaven.

Through fleshly veil, in gentler light,
  And temper'd Deity,
He loves, in pity infinite,
  To lay His terrors by,
Fitting His glories to our weaker sight.

That, rock-engraven, firm and true,
  Gave but the stern command;
This, heart-impress'd, for ever new,
  And writ not with the hand,
Doth give with the command the power
    to do.

In silent characters that stood;
  These, with a gentle sway,
With living voice and actions good,
  Themselves first led the way,
And sealèd with the seal of their own blood.

O Thou, who didst Thy saints incline
  The words of life to bear,
Prepare our souls to be Thy shrine,
  And with Thy finger there
Write Thine own laws in characters Divine.

Train Thou us, Lord, with Thee to die,
  That we from death may rise,
Our steps on earth, our hearts on high,
  Our treasure in the skies,
Where God Triune doth reign for ever nigh.

Commemoration of a Martyr.

AT THE FIRST VESPERS.

" Have not I commanded thee? be strong and of a good
courage: be not afraid, neither be thou dismayed, for the
Lord thy God is with thee whithersoever thou goest."
—*Joshua* i.

Ex quo salus mortalium.

Our Lord the path of suffering trod,
  And since His sacred blood hath flowed,
'Tis meet that man should yield to God
        The life he owed.

No shame to own the Crucified,
  Nay, 'tis our immortality
That we confess our God who died,
        And for Him die.

Fill'd with this thought with patient smile
  Threat'ning and death he doth withstand,
Fights, Lord, Thy cause, and leans the while
        Upon Thine hand.

Seeing above the golden crown,
  Into death's arms he willing goes;
Dying, he conquers death; o'erthrown,
        O'erthrows his foes.

Thus one doth vanquish strong-arm'd
    bands,
And o'er his torturers mightier rise,
'Till e'en the judge astonish'd stands
        With awe-struck eyes.

Lord, make us Thine own soldiers true,
    That we may gain the spirit pure,
And for Thy Name, Thy Cross in view,
        All things endure.

Eternal Father of the Word,
    Eternal Son, we Thee adore,
Eternal Spirit, God and Lord,
        For evermore.

AT MIDNIGHT.

"Whosoever will save his life shall lose it; but whosoever shall lose his life for My sake and the Gospel's, the
same shall save it."—*Mark* viii.

Felix morte tuâ, qui cruciatibus.

How happy the mortal,
    Through pains and dismay,
Who hath burst the portal
    To regions of day.

Where death hath benighted,
    Ere life's sun went down,
The faith that he plighted,
    With death he doth crown.

Our weak spirits languish
  At sound of death's feet,
But thou the stern anguish
  Dost go forth to meet.

Yet nothing confounded,
  With rack and with chains,
Where death hath abounded
  With tortures and pains.

Lo, from highest Heaven,
  His champion to own,
Between the clouds riven,
  Is Christ looking down.

His band hath He holden,
  Where weak nature fails;
His Spirit doth embolden,
  And in him prevails.

Shall we then soft-hearted
  Seek ease and repose,
And sing the departed
  In death and stern woes?

Let such themes of wonder
  Arouse us from sleep,
Lest, woke by death's thunder
  We wake but to weep.

Great Father, Son, Spirit,
  The Ancient of days,
May we Thee inherit,
  And sing of Thy praise.

AT THE MATTINS.

" He that overcometh, the same shall be clothed in white raiment; and I will not blot out his name out of the book of life, but I will confess his name before My Father, and before His angels."—Rev. iii.

Jam non te lacerant carnificum manus.

Fear no more for the torturer's hand,
  Nor the dungeon dark that bound thee;
The choirs of Heaven about thee stand,
  Bright shining homes surround thee.

Fear no more for the clanking chain,
  Thou art free as light of Heaven;
The stripes that mark'd thy frame with pain,
  For rays of thy crown are given.

Fear no more for stern cold, nor need,
  Nor for nakedness for ever;
Christ's pure light doth clothe thee and feed,
  And shall no more from thee sever.

Lo, He stands at His martyr's side,
  Death with nobler life surrounding,
And takes him with Him to abide,
  The dread tyrant's wrath confounding.

To God on high be honour done,
  In the height all height exceeding;
To Father, Son, and Holy One,
  From Father and Son proceeding.

Commemoration of many Martyrs.

AT MIDNIGHT.

" These are they which came out of great tribulation : and have washed their robes, and made them white in the blood of the Lamb."—Rev. vii.

Fortes cadendo martyres.

Of the martyrs we sing,
  Whom the purple adorns ;
Who have followed their King
  In His dread crown of thorns.

Now their storms are all past,
  And their dark sea of blood
Hath conveyed them, at last,
  To their haven of good.

Though the tyrant is stern,
  Yet they fear not his rod,
For their fears nought discern
  But the terrors of God.

Where fierce foemen pursue,
  Their life-blood they afford,
As an offering due
  To their suffering Lord.

With His own martyrs' blood,
   Then His blood also pleads,
Which once flow'd on the wood,—
   And for them intercedes.

Thus the woe which remains
   Must Christ's body fulfil,
Till the last drop it drains
   In His cup of all ill.

He for us who was spent,
   In His fulness complete,
Shall Himself then present,
   For His Father made meet.

Dread Jehovah, we sing,
   In Christ Jesus made known :
Of all martyrs the King,
   Of all martyrs the Crown.

AT THE MATTINS.

"Blessed are they which are persecuted for righteousness'
sake, for theirs is the kingdom of Heaven."—Matt. i.

Quam, Christe, signasti viam.

O Christ, on the dark way where Thou art
    leading,
   Mark'd with Thy blood falling upon the
    ground,
Thy soldiers, gazing on Thee, are proceeding,
   And, warring in Thy strength, with Thee are
    found.

Pierced in hands, and pierced in feet,
Thou dost take Thy starry seat,
Thither Thy wounded martyrs flee,
As on the narrow road they follow Thee.

Around Thy judgment-seat they are assem-
bling,
Clothed in their robes of blood, and in their
need
They show their gory wounds, in silent trem-
bling,
Eloquent mouths which for Thy pity plead.
Lord, while martyrs trembling stand
For Thy final dread command,
And canst Thou us Thy suppliants own,
Low to the ground by guilty crimes weigh'd
down ?

We drink not of Thy cup in their full measure,
But there are worse than cruel tyrants' arts ;
O, let no wiles of self-destroying pleasure
Melt down in reckless ruin our weak hearts :
That unto Thee, our God and King,
We may ever praises sing ;
The Father, and eternal Word,
And the eternal Spirit, God and Lord.

Commemoration of Bishops.

"No man taketh this honour unto himself, but he that
is called of God, as was Aaron. So also Christ glorified
not Himself to be made an High Priest; but He that said
unto Him, Thou art My Son, to-day have I begotten Thee.
As He saith also in another place, Thou art a Priest for
ever, after the order of Melchisedec."—*Heb.* v.

Christe, pastorum caput atque princeps.

O CHRIST, the chief of Pastors, Head and
   Crown,
 The Head on which the anointing came of
   yore,
And to the mantle's skirts went softly down,
 This day to Thy true priest the witness bore.

He, who with no self-will, nor spirit vain,
 Nor impious self-confidence made bold,
Hath dared that fearful and dread seat sustain,
 But bidden of his Lord His staff to hold.

His Champion true, to wage His heavenly war,
 The Spirit hath anointed all within,
From His full horn of blessings; and from far
 Hath sent His flock to feed, and souls to win.

Shepherd, and Father, and example fair,
 His all he spends for them —himself is spent ;

Servant of servants, weighed by others' care,
   And all things made to all men,—wholly
      bent

Lost souls to save, he for the guilty prays,
   Comforts the comfortless, instructs the blind;
Walks amid loftier thoughts than human ways,
   With heaven-wrought chains the evil foe to
      bind.

Grant, Lord, his prayers may not be all in
      vain,—
   That we a royal priesthood may be won;
And, with an ever freshly-flowing strain,
   May sing the Father, Spirit, and the Son!

AT MIDNIGHT.

"Who is a faithful and wise servant whom His Lord hath made ruler over His household, to give them meat in due season? Blessed is that servant whom His Lord when He cometh shall find so doing."—*Matt.* xxiv.

Christe, decreto Patris institutus.

CHRIST, by Thy Father's high decree,
   Seal'd the great Priest to be,
Who choosest Thine own ministry,
   And formest them to Thee.
Where shall we find a faithful breast,
   Meet for Thy high behest?
Fit worldly meed by worth to claim,
   A lov'd and honour'd name:

Yet loath and weeping doth he stand,
  Led by Thy guiding hand,
To take from Thee the pastor's crown,
  And terrible renown.
Well taught the dangers that surround,
  That high and heavenly ground,
Beneath the absorbing cares to groan,
  Of all men but his own.
By fervent love unquiet made,
  On every need of aid,
To his dear flock he instant flies
  On wings of charities;
He shews the way, and he precedes,
  It is his life that leads;
And while his words the faith reveal,
  His actions set the seal,
God's house is fragrant with the breath
  Of Christ's life-giving death.
The lame man's staff, the blind man's sight,
  The sinner's guiding light,
A Father, prompt to hear each call,
  And all things made to all!
Pastor of pastors, who didst bleed
  With Thee Thy flock to feed,
May we Thy pastures evermore
  Attain by Thee the door!

AT THE MATTINS.

"Feed the flock of God which is among you, taking the oversight thereof not by constraint, but willingly; not for filthy lucre but of a ready mind: neither as being lords over God's heritage, but being ensamples to the flock." —*1 Pet. v.*

Jesu, Sacerdotum decus.

Jesu, who didst Thy pastor crown,
And let this day Thy blessing down,
    Hear us, we pray!
Thou art Thyself the Diadem,
Brightening with many a living gem,
    And heavenly ray.

Proof of his love, and pledge of Thine,
He bears the mission from Thy shrine,
    Thy staff to hold;—
The charge of Thine own ransom'd sheep,
Which Thee the Father gave to keep,—
    And guard Thy fold.

He knows them all, of them is known,
He knows and goes before his own,
    By stream and rock,
To lead, and shelter'd pastures give;
They hear, they follow, and they live,
    A gentle flock.

When one hath wander'd from his sight,
He seeketh it, both day and night,
    The mountains round;

And joy repayeth all his fears,
When to the fold he homeward bears
    The lost and found.

The roaring beasts he sets afar,
And wolves that with more treacherous war
    Come prowling nigh;
Their guileful arts he knows full well—
Ready with his dear flock to dwell,
    For them to die.

Oft, as the unbloody sacrifice
He offers up, of countless price,
    And shares the feast,
Himself he on the altar lays,
And his own flock, with prayer and praise,
    A holy Priest.

All praise to Thee, the Priest supreme,
Through whom alone all blessings stream,
    Th' Eternal Son;
And may Thy ransom'd heritage
Thy glory sing from age to age,
    God, Three in One,

Commemoration of Doctors.

AT THE FIRST VESPERS.

"God giveth wisdom unto the wise, and knowledge to
them that know understanding. He revealeth the deep and
secret things; He knoweth what is in the darkness, and
the light dwelleth with Him."—Dan. ii.

O qui perpetuus nos Monitor doces.

O THOU, our only Teacher and true Friend,
  Hid from our sight in mansions of the sky,
How dost Thou from Thy Father's bosom send
  Kind guides, who may Thy leading hand
    supply.

Such as keep holy watch, lest aught should
    stain
  Th' unsullied virgin bloom, which must be-
    long
Unto the ancient faith, doom'd to remain
  In undefilèd lustre ever young.

To beat down idol towers of Canaan old,
  And pestilential errors drive away;
To bear Christ's little ones back to the fold,
  Whom heresy to wilds hath led astray.

Ye sires of hoary eld, serenely stern,
  Faith throws a light upon the path ye trod ;
Things old ye teach, things new ye overturn,
  And keep the dread deposit of your God.

Thus, Truth, tho' thou be voiceless, yet thy
      word
  Goes through the world, and speaks in every
      part
Converting all, while not a sound is heard,
  Teaching, through ancient sires, the meek
      in heart.

AT MIDNIGHT.

"Happy is the man that findeth wisdom, and the man
that getteth understanding. For the merchandise of it is
better than the merchandise of silver, and the gain thereof
than fine gold. She is more precious than rubies : and all
the things thou canst desire are not to be compared unto
her."—*Prov.* iii.

Jam nunc, quæ numeras tot tibi vindices.

GENTLY lift thy starry head,
    Lift thy head, Religion, now ;
Every dart against Thee sped
    Is a laurel on thy brow.
When wild rage is on thee set,
    Then Thy martyrs go before ;
When dark error lays her net,
    Learned sons hast Thou in store.

They the rising plague descry,
  When the gangrene spreads abroad;
When the night comes on the sky,
  They are stars about our road.
To the weak, strength, light, and ease;
  Shipwreck'd barks to shore they turn;
To us, sailing the dark seas,
  Like unfailing lights they burn.

May our lives their teaching prove;
  May their words with Thine agree;
While we them revere and love,
  In them may we follow Thee.
Then Thy praise shall rise around,
  Truth, whose spirit-speaking tongue
Goeth forth with voiceless sound,
  And deep hearts the notes prolong.

AT THE MATTINS.

"They that be wise shall shine as the brightness of the firmament; and they that turn many to righteousness, as the stars, for ever and ever."—*Dan.* xii.

Vos succensa Deo splendida lumina.

HAIL, glorious lights, kindled at God's own
    urn,
Salt of the nations—whence the soul imbue
Savours of Godhead, virtues pure and true,
So that all die not—whence serenely burn
In their bright orbs sure Truth and Virtue
    bold,

Putting on virgin honours undefiled :
Bounteous by you, the world's Deliverer mild
Of treasur'd wisdom deals His stores untold.
Hail ! channels where the living waters flow,
Whence the Redeemer's field shews fair, and
    glow
The golden harvests : ye, from realms above,
Bring meat for manly hearts, and milk for
    babes in love.
These bear, great God, Thy sword and shield ;
These rear th' eternal palace hall ;
Skill'd with one hand Thine arms to wield,
    With one to build Thy wall.

Ye, in your bright celestial panoply,
    Overcame dark heresy :
And when her brood from Stygian night
    Renew the fight,
We too may grasp your arrows bright ;
E'en till this hour we combat in your mail,
And with no doubtful end,—we combat and
    prevail.
Hail ! Heavenly Truth, guiding the pen
    Of wise and holy men ;
To thee, though thou be voiceless, doth belong
    A spirit's tongue,
Which in the heart's deep home uttereth a song.

Commemoration of Presbyters.

AT THE FIRST AND SECOND VESPERS.

"Blessed is the man whom Thou choosest, and receivest
unto Thee; he shall dwell in Thy courts, and shall be satis-
fied with the pleasures of Thy house, even of Thy holy
temple."—*Ps. lxv. 5.*

Quantis micas honoribus.

Good Priest, where art thou hid from human
      eyes
    In calm repose,
Haply to tread the marble-shining skies
    After life's woes;
Where God's own presence hath His people
      blest,
Himself their happy guerdon, and their rest.

Those virtues, in whose steps thou here didst
      toil,
    And strive to go,
Are not put off with this thy fleshly coil,
    And left below;
They now are turn'd to rays of light Divine,
And glorious crowns, which on thy temples
      shine.

And they for whom thou toil'dst in second
      birth,
    With many a sigh,
Are with thee like thy children, fled from
      earth,
    And through the sky
They share thy victory the blest choirs among,
And lift with thee the new mysterious song.

Thou here below, dim-veil'd from earthly eyes,
    In shadows dread,
Didst offer up th' unbloody sacrifice,
    On Christ to feed;
He now Himself, with unveil'd Deity,
Of spirits immortal the repast shall be.

And as a daily sacrifice may we
    Be lifted up,
Bearing our daily Cross, and share with thee
    Thy Master's cup:
We press, like shipwreck'd sailors on the wave,
To shores where Christ doth stretch His arms
      to save.

To Him, who governs His own priestly host,
    Himself their crown;
To Him, with Father and with Holy Ghost,
    Be all renown;
All praise to Him as hath been heretofore,
All praise to Him both now and evermore.

AT MIDNIGHT.

"Who shall ascend into the hill of the Lord; or who
shall rise up in His holy place? Even he that hath clean
hands and a pure heart."—*Ps. xxiv.*

Jam satis fluxit cruor hostiarum.

ENOUGH the blood of victims flow'd of old,
   The shadows pass, and legal offerings ;
Now higher ministries, Thou, Lord, dost mould,
   On which a holier shade Thy Priesthood
      flings.

Elias from the heavens call'd down the flame ;
   One greater than Elias, hid from sight,
Is here, obedient to His awful name,
   Of Him we make the dread memorial rite.

Great office, the mysterious cup to bear
   In which the guilty world's salvation lies,
And with our trembling hands, full of deep
      fear,
   To offer up the bloodless sacrifice.

O more than all to ancient prophets given,
   More than to angels, if but understood,
That in our trembling hands the God of Heaven
   Doth give Himself to be the spirit's food.

Grant, Christ, that we, fulfilling Thy com-
  mands,
Of Thy blest presence may approach the seat,
With hearts by Thee made pure, and holy
  hands ;
May love for Thy dread altars make us meet.

Son of the eternal Father, God above,
May all the world beneath Thy feet adore,
Who sendest down the Spirit, with Thy love
Thy Priesthood to anoint for evermore.

AT THE MATTINS.

" No man taketh this honour unto himself, but he that
is called of God, as was Aaron."—*Heb.* v.

O sacerdotum veneranda jura.

AWFUL is the priestly state,
 Which, by faith beheld aright,
Closes and unbars the gate,
 Though unseen by mortal sight.
Christ, in this His earthly seat,
Holds in them the balance meet,
Binds and lets the sinner's feet
 In His own appointed rite.

When they ply their healing art,
 'Tis His hand in them is found ;
When they soothe the wounded heart,
 His anointing heals the wound.

When they speak, the faithful sheep
Drink their words and hide them deep,
For the law of God they steep
  First in their own hearts profound.

When the wrath is going forth,
  And the vial in mid air,
They stand forth to stop the wrath
  With deep importuning prayer.
May they, Lord, themselves be wise,
Who touch Thy dread mysteries,
Mirrors, in their people's eyes,
  Worthy of the things they bear.

Father, Spirit, Son Divine,
  Who dost rescue from the grave,
From Heaven's central echoing shrine
  Let Thy glory, wave on wave,
Fill the all-surrounding sea
Of shoreless eternity,
Singing, Priest of Priests, of Thee,
  And Thy mighty power to save.

Commemoration of Abbots, Monks, and Anchorites.

AT THE FIRST VESPERS.

"Come out from among them, and be ye separate, saith
the Lord, and touch not the unclean thing; and I will receive you, and will be a Father unto you, and ye shall be
my sons and daughters, saith the Lord Almighty."—2 Cor. vi.

Felices nemorum pangimus incolas.

HAPPY are they whom God's protecting love,
   From out the world's contagious influence,
Hath hid, as in some calm and sheltering grove,
   In sweet designs of holiest Providence.

With heart that seeks for Thee, for Thee
      which longs,
   City, and home, and friends, themselves they
      leave;
For poor is all which to this earth belongs,
   To them who try to know what they believe.

The wrestler, who an earthly crown would gain,
   Casts each besetting care and weight behind;
The mariner, to cross the distant main,
   Gives thoughts of rest and softness to the
      wind.

For wealth that lasts, and joys that cannot
    fail,
  They every fading trifle cast aside,
With sound true heart, if so they may prevail,
  Trusting in hopes which with their God
    abide.

Therefore their glory is to be despised,
  And all their wealth is cheerful poverty;
Thus best they find what they have mostly
    prized,
  Their consolation daily death to die.

Grant, Lord, that we with sooth'd and sooth-
    ing mind,
  May take the penalties to sinners due,
Wean'd from the world, and to its ills resign'd,
  Building our trust in mansions ever true.

Glory to God the Father, Thee we call;
  Glory to God the Son who sits above;
Glory to Thee, Great Spirit, holding all,
  Great Spirit, holding all in bonds of love.

AT THE MATTINS.

"The multitude of them that believed were of one heart
and of one soul; neither said any of them that ought of
the things which he possessed was his own; but they had
all things common."—*Acts* iv.

O pulchras acies, castraque fortia.

Fair camp in arms of peaceful fortitude,
  And no ungentle warfare, in one band
Together knit of holy brotherhood,—

    One faith, one hope, one Leader, sternly
          train'd,
Far from earth's noise, to learn the eternal
          song,
    And gain the conquest of a heavenly land.

By prayer, and holy plaints which Heaven's
          gate throng,
  And discipline of penitential ways,
The flesh is weaken'd, but the soul is strong.

    Each for himself, and each for other prays,
All for God's Church; thus, in blest union,
    The strength of interwoven shields they
          raise

To storm the citadel, high Mercy's throne;—
  No unapprovèd violence, for so
The Father of all goodness would be won.

Then, 'tween the clouds the covenanted bow
Opens, a glorious city to disclose,
  Where angels to their aid pass to and fro.

When fervid day with busy tumult glows,
  Their voice is heard not; but when tranquil
    even
Comes on, with stillness of the night's repose,

  And the world sleeps, their voice is heard in
    Heaven.
Thus self-denial girds the homeward soul;
  And feeble knees, to prayer and watching
    given,

Gain strength; the eye is cleans'd to see the
    goal;
  Not idle, nor by others' toils supplied;
Thus conscience takes the reins of self-control,

  And her lost regal strength, to sway the tide
Of roving and wild thoughts, herself made free,
  By taking of Christ's yoke, releas'd from
    pride

Of her own heart; releas'd from vanity;
  Glad to receive what God thinks good to
    give,
Sole charter of celestial liberty.

  To speak the Father's glory all things strive,
And all, co-equal Son, to speak of Thee,
  And Thee, good Spirit, by whose breath we
    live.

THE ANCHORITE.

"The world is crucified unto me, and I unto the
world." —Gal. vi.

Quid tu relictis urbibus.

Why dost thou flee the peopled seat?
Why love the shade and dim retreat?
What seest thou in that silent mood
Conversing with the solitude?

Thus soars the soul on freer wing
To mansions of unfading spring;
And less to earthly influence given,
Her meditation holds with Heaven.

In quietness of sacred love
They present seem with choirs above;
Their thoughts with God for evermore,
To know, to worship, and adore.

What joys Thou dost to them impart,
Who serve Thee, Lord, with stedfast heart!
They seek for Thee the cave unblest;
Thou hid'st them in Thy fostering breast.

Glory to God both Three and One,
The Father, Spirit, and the Son,
The exceeding great reward art Thou
Of them who strive Thy love to know.

Commemoration of Just Men.

AT THE VESPERS.

Summi pusillus grex Patris.

Be not afraid, ye little flock,
  Though poor and profitless your lives,
Let not distrust your sorrows mock,
  A Father's love the kingdom gives.

Lo, now there reigns among the blest,
  Who once was like yourselves below,—
By self-abasement and unrest
  Christ's wisdom taught in school of woe.

In penitence his soul to save,
  He fix'd his eyes on Him before,
Where, through life's dim and shadowy cave,
  His Lord the bleeding burden bore.

Upon his lips did love preside,
  Or silence sit with charity :
In lap of want he lov'd to hide
  What he would to himself deny.

His food it was the heavenly word;
  He search'd the Book of Truth and Love,
Till watchful prayer would wings afford,
  And he would be with them above.

This is the narrow way to heaven;
  O holy Godhead, holy Three,
The Three in One, to us be given,
  Thus by this way to come to Thee.

AT MIDNIGHT.

"He said to them all, If any man will come after Me, let him deny himself, and take up his cross daily and follow Me."—Luke ix.

Non parta solo sanguine.

Nor by the martyr's death alone
The martyr's crown in heaven is won;
There is a triumph robe on high
For bloodless fields of victory.

What though not taught the flame to feel,
The lions' den, the torturing wheel;
Himself his only enemy,
He learns a living death to die.

What though nor executioner,
Nor scourge, nor stake, nor chains be there,
To those prepared with Christ to die,
'Tis all supplied with charity.

The rebel flesh when self-control
Hath tamed, and faith the wayward soul,
Love, with her torch-light from the skies,
Shall fire the holy sacrifice.

The veins all ope, life's stream hath stood,
Ready to flow, love mastering fears,
But finding not its way, the blood
Hath turn'd, and shed itself in tears.

Grant, Christ, that so to Thee we turn,
That we to die through life may learn ;
And thus beyond brief life with Thee
May see a glad eternity.

Eternal Father of the Word,
Eternal Son, as God adored,
Eternal Spirit, equal Three,
Be equal glory given to Thee !

AT THE MATTINS.

"Our rejoicing is this, the testimony of our conscience,
that in simplicity and godly sincerity, not with fleshly
wisdom, but by the grace of God, we have had our conversation in the world, and more abundantly to you-ward."
—2 Cor. i.

Qui te, Deus, sub intimo.

Who Thee receives in secret breast,
   And makes his soul Thy sanctuary,
This is to him no place of rest ;
   He, self-forgotten, looks to Thee.

O Lord, why hast Thou us delay'd
  So long, in hope's dim prison pent ?
Thou citizens of heaven hast made,
  And earth is place of banishment.

'Tis that love's lamp may purer glow,
  Our sensual spirits to refine,
Hastening to heaven, that here below
  We may be dead to all but Thine.

That feeling weight of this dull earth,
  The soul may long her wing to free,
Preparing for a better birth,
  Hid in Thy boundless majesty.

Eternal Sire, Eternal Word,
  Eternal Spirit, equal Three,
For ever in one God adored,
  Be equal glory given to Thee.

Commemoration of Virgins.

AT THE FIRST VESPERS.

" Every man hath his proper gift of God, one after this manner, and another after that. I say therefore to the unmarried and widows, it is good for them if they so abide."—1 Cor. vii.

Vos O virginei cum citharis chori.

Ye Virgin company
Who tune your golden harps on high,
True to the Lamb in trial's hour,
And now His flock's celestial flower,
Rising through gate of heavenly morn,
  Sing ye the Virgin-born !

  This is the sacred day
When first He call'd you hence away,
When with your full-orb'd lamps of light,
Ye summon'd were at dead of night;
And now ye stand beside His throne,
  For ever made His own.

  Ye kept from earthly fire
That holier love might you inspire ;
And when yourselves your Lord's to be
Ye bound in stern fidelity,
He more and more did bind the chain,
  And aye with you remain.

Lest worldly image, brought
O'er the pure mirror of your thought,
Should sully the heaven-opening soul,
Which ye to God devoted whole ;
Your mind upon itself was driven,
  Your eye and ear in heaven.

And thus the flesh subdued
Put on a gradual hardihood,
Till, dying day by day away,
Ye cheated death of half its prey,
That while ye wait His heavenly call,
  God might be all in all.

Such is the Virgin soul
Wedded on earth to Christ's control ;
May we that pureness emulate ;
Bound to Thee, Lord, in holiest state
We are a sacred nation, we should be
  Living alone to Thee.

Almighty Father, grant
We ever may Thy glory chaunt ;
Christ, may we in that company
Where'er Thou goest follow Thee :
Good Spirit, ever pure and bold,
  Light Thou our bosoms cold.

AT MIDNIGHT.

" At midnight there was a cry made, Behold, the Bridegroom cometh; go ye out to meet Him. Then all those virgins arose and trimmed their lamps."—*Matt.* xxv.

Cœlestis aula panditur.

OPEN is the starry hall ;
Hear ye ? 'tis the Bridegroom's call !
Holy Virgins, one and all,
    Ready stand,
For the heavenly festival
    Is at hand !

Come at last the nuptial day,
Tears for ever pass'd away ;
Fled the prison-house, the clay,
    And the thrall ;
God for ever your sure stay,
    And your all !

In His presence is the store,
Purest joys for evermore,
And the fountain flowing o'er :
    No more night,
Safe upon the happy shore
    Of the light !

What fleet pleasure's fading bower
    And control?
God's own presence is the dower
    Of the soul!

Wondrous, glorious mystery,
When the soul from flesh is free!
Bond of sweetness which shall be
    When the heart
Join'd is to Deity,
    Ne'er to part!

Praise to Thee, Almighty One,
Triune Father, Spirit, Son,
By whose boundless grace alone
    Spirits know
Heaven's immortal union
    E'en below.

AT THE SECOND VESPERS.

"Hearken, O daughter, and consider; incline thine ear:
forget also thine own people, and thy Father's house."
—Psalm xlv.

Non vana dilectum gregem.

THE flock belov'd, no worldly joy
    Hath fed with vanities;
Nor earthly image dimm'd the breast,
    Reflecting the pure skies.

A higher thought, a nobler aim,
  The Virgin soul employs;
Which nothing else but Thee, O Lord,
  But Thee in all enjoys.

With more than wedded charities
  Then Thou to them dost turn,
And in their bosom all unfelt
  With thoughts divine dost burn.

They, touch'd by that transforming power,
  Put on mysterious change;
Nor, knowing, know their blessedness,
  In union new and strange.

Then suppliant we pray Thee, Lord,
  That no contagious dart
Should influence our sense, and, through
  The senses, reach the heart!

Praise God, the Father, Spirit, Son,
  Who doth Himself reveal,
And sets on souls that He hath won
  His love's transforming seal.

AT THE SECOND VESPERS.

O virgo pectus cui sacrum.

O THOU, upon whose breast no earthly flame
Importunate with passionate sorrows came;
But Spirit hath alighted, calmly pure,
With better hopes for ever to endure.

Soft pleasure's soul-pervading influence
Ne'er unnerv'd thy stern purpose, wean'd
    from sense
To seek for worthier bridals, and below
The Lamb to follow wheresoe'er He go.

For the dread Virgin-born, ineffable
In His eternal beauty, so did fill
Thy soul, that thou didst tread on earthly care,
Walking on high, nor rival thought couldst
    bear.

Now knowest thou that blessedness, while o'er
Heaven's multitudinous voices thine doth soar
In sweetness, singing while the Bridegroom's
    brow
Shines o'er thee, singing through the eternal
    Now.

O Jesu, God eternal, gently prove,
And teach us how to praise Thee !   Thou that
    love
Dost only to the pure in heart disclose,
Which Thee, the Father, and the Spirit knows.

Commemoration of Holy Women.

AT THE FIRST VESPERS.

"A man shall leave his father and mother, and shall be joined unto his wife, and they two shall be one flesh. This is a great mystery: but I speak concerning Christ and the Church. Nevertheless let every one of you in particular so love his wife even as himself; and the wife see that she reverence her husband."—*Ephes.* v.

Ad nuptias Agni Pater.

To the Lamb's festival
God doth His people call;
Blest she who hears that nuptial song,
And sits those guests among.

Love is her bridal tie,
Her dower is poverty;
'Mid earthly clouds she heavenward springs,
And treads on human things.

Stern hardihood she wears,
And penitential tears,
With fasting girt, as with a zone,
Her heavenly race to run.

Unto the Crucified
She looks, like faithful bride,
Prepared, where'er He lead the way,
To suffer and obey.

Blest they, whom God above
Doth bind with cords of love :
Them shall the heavenly Bridegroom own,
    In soul and body one.

This union grant to me
'Thrice Holy, One and Three :
Ye fill the universe so wide,
    But with the meek abide !

AT MIDNIGHT.

"Who can find a virtuous woman? for her price is far
above rubies. The heart of her husband doth safely trust
her. She will do him good and not evil all the days of her
life."—*Prov. xxxi.*

Adeste, sanctæ conjuges.

Come, behold a holy grave
    Of one in virtue brave,
Whom Faith and Love, though here so dim,
Now clothe with wings of seraphim.

By insidious follies woo'd,
    She put on fortitude,
And beauty that doth flow from Thee,
Soul of indwelling piety.

Where the world would weave her thrall,
    She fled the glittering pall,
Lest Pleasure, with her arts refined,
Should gradual gain the unwary mind.

Hers was not the adorning
Of plait, or gold, or ring,
But meekly clad, in spirit free,
Of unadorn'd simplicity.

'Neath her looks serene conceal'd
Stern virtue hid her shield,
Fearing to lose that love within,
Which half is lost by being seen.

Lingering at the heavenly door,
Her food was holy lore;
Still daily in the courts of prayer,
Still glad her household toils to share.

All doth flow from Thy great urn;
All doth to Thee return;
The praise be Thine, Eternal Three,
As was, and is, and aye shall be!

AT THE MATTINS.

"Ye wives, be in subjection to your own husbands; that
if any obey not the word, they also may without the word
be won by the conversation of the wives; while they behold
your chaste conversation coupled with fear."—1 *Pet.* iii.

Ardet Deo quæ fœmina.

She strove, but strove in vain, that love to
hide,
The flame that burn'd within to God and
Heaven;

For meek-eyed Poverty was at her side,
  And many a tongue to lowly deeds hath
  given !

Her only care to follow her dear Lord,
  Servant of servants, where on life's dim road
Her temper'd ray calm Duty did afford,
  Or Love hath led the way to doing good.

Hid 'neath the garb of lowly poverty,
  Oft cherish'd she her Lord, and knew it not :
Harsh to herself, to others kind and free,—
  Ah, not untaught to feel affliction's lot.

At home—abroad—in words of holy care,
  Or more endearing silence, breathing peace,
Seeking all hearts to bind with heavenly fear,
  And bid the unholy sounds of discord cease.

Not unto us, Eternal Sire of Heaven,
  Not unto us the praise, Eternal Son,
Not unto us—to Thee be glory given,
  To Thee, Eternal Spirit, Three in One !

In the Office of the Consecration of a Church.

AT THE FIRST VESPERS.

Urbs Jerusalem beata.

THE holy Jerusalem
From highest Heaven descending,
  And crown'd with a diadem
Of Angel bands attending,
The Living City built on high
Bright with "celestial jewelry."

  She comes the bride, from heaven gate,
In nuptial new adorning,
  To meet the Immaculate,
Like coming of the morning.
Her streets of purest gold are made,
Her walls a diamond palisade.

  There with pearls the gates are dight
Upon that holy mountain ;
  And thither come both day and night,
Who in the Living Fountain

Have wash'd their robes from earthly stain,
And borne below Christ's lowly chain.

By the hand of the Unknown
The Living Stones are moulded
To a glorious shrine, all one,
Full soon to be unfolded :
The building wherein God doth dwell,
The Holy Church invisible.

Glory be to God, who laid
In Heaven the foundation ;
And to the Spirit, who hath made
The walls of our salvation ;
To Christ, Himself the Corner Stone,
Be glory ! to the Three in One.

AT MIDNIGHT.

"And I heard a great voice out of heaven, saying, Behold the tabernacle of God is with men, and He will dwell with them."—*Rev.* xxi.

Angularis fundamentum.

CHRIST is set the corner-stone,
And the sole foundation,
And a City springs thereon,
Sion's holy nation ;
Builded in the Three in One,
In divinest union.

See, belov'd of God to be,
　　Its high head it raises,
Fill'd with vocal jubilee,
　　And celestial praises ;
　The Eternal One and Three
　Singing everlastingly.

In Thy temple from above
　　Come and take thy dwelling,
With the greatness of thy love
　　Highest heaven excelling ;
　From Thy fountain here renew
　Thy life-giving heavenly dew !

Here, whene'er they seek Thy strength,
　　Hallow their endeavour
In Thee to be built at length,
　　To abide for ever ;
　And, translated from our eyes,
　Rest with Thee in paradise !

Christ is the true corner-stone,
　　And the sole foundation,
Let the city built thereon,
　　Sion's holy nation,
　Ever praise the Three in One,
　Join'd in holiest union.

AT THE MATTINS.

"Surely the Lord is in this place .... How dreadful is
this place! this is none other but the house of God, and
this is the gate of heaven."—*Gen.* xxviii.

Patris æterni soboles coæva.

O WORD of God above,
Who fillest all in all,
Hallow this house with Thy sure love,
And bless our festival.

There dwells in this deep fount
Anointing souls to lave,
And from beneath this holy mount
Goes forth the healing wave.

Here Christ, of His own blood,
Himself the chalice gives,
And feeds His own with angels' food,
On which the Spirit lives.

For guilty souls that pine
Sure mercies here abound,
And healing grace, with oil and wine,
For every secret wound.

God from His throne afar,
Comes in this house to dwell ;
And prayer, beyond the evening star,
Builds here her citadel.

No wintry storm nor shower
    Shall harm this holy home,
Nor, worse than they, the evil power
    Which dwells within the gloom.

All might, all praise be Thine,
    The God whom all adore,
The Father, Son, and Spirit Divine,
    Both now and evermore.

AT THE SECOND VESPERS.

"Lord, who shall dwell in Thy tabernacle: or who shall rest upon Thy holy hill? Even he that leadeth an uncorrupt life: and doeth the thing which is right, and speaketh the truth from his heart."—*Psalm xv.*

Ecce sedes hic Tonantis.

This is the abode where God doth dwell,
    This is the gate of Heaven,
The shrine of the Invisible,
    The Priest, the Victim given,
Our God Himself content to die,
In boundless charity.

O holy seat, O holy fane,
    Where dwells the Omnipotent,
Whom the broad world cannot contain,
    Nor heaven's high firmament.
He visits earth's poor sky-roof'd cell,
And here He deigns to dwell.

Here, where the unearthly Guest de-
scends
To hearts of innocence,
And sacred love her wing extends
Of holiest influence,—
He 'mid His children loves to be
In lowly majesty.

Let no unhallow'd thought be here
Within that sacred door ;
Let nought polluted dare draw near,
Nor tread the awful floor ;
For lo, the Avenger is at hand,
And at the door doth stand !

To Thee, ne'er ending, ne'er begun,
Thrice holy Trinity,
Father, and Son, and Spirit—One,
For ever glory be ;
Anointing for Thy dwelling-place
The living shrines of grace.

FROM THE PARISIAN MISSAL.

"Out of the deep have I called unto Thee, O Lord;
Lord, hear my voice: O let Thine ears consider well the
voice of my complaint. If Thou, Lord, wilt be extreme
to mark what is done amiss, O Lord, who may abide it ?"
—*Psalm* cxxx.

Dies iræ, dies illa.

DAY of wrath !—that awful day
Shall the banner'd Cross display,
Earth in ashes melt away !

The trembling, the agony,
When His coming shall be nigh,
Who shall all things judge and try

When the trumpet's thrilling tone,
Through the tombs of ages gone,
Summons all before the throne.

Death and Time shall stand aghast,
And Creation, at the blast,
Rise, to answer for the past.

Then the volume shall be spread,
And the writing shall be read,
Which shall judge the quick and dead !

Then the Judge shall sit ! oh then !
All that's hid shall be made plain,
Unrequited nought remain.

What shall wretched I then plead ?
Who for me shall intercede,
When the righteous scarce is freed ?

King of dreadful Majesty,
Saving souls in mercy free,
Fount of Pity, save Thou me !

Bear me, Lord, in heart I pray,
Object of Thy saving way,
Lest Thou lose me on that day.

Weary seeking me wast Thou,
And for me in death didst bow,
Be Thy toils availing now !

Judge of Justice, Thee, I pray,
Grant me pardon while I may,
Ere that awful reckoning-day.

O'er my crimes I guilty groan,
Blush to think what I have done,
Spare Thy suppliant, Holy One.

Thou didst set the adultress free,
Heard'st the thief upon the tree—
Hope vouchsafing e'en to me.

Nought of Thee my prayers can claim,
Save in Thy free mercy's name,
Save me from the deathless flame !

With Thy sheep my place assign,
Separate from th' accursed line,
Set me on Thy right hand with Thine.

When the lost, to silence driven,
To devouring flames are given,
Call me with the blest to Heaven !

Suppliant, fallen, low I bend,
My bruised heart to ashes rend,
Care Thou, Lord, for my last end !

Full of tears that day shall prove
When, from ashes rising, move

To the judgment guilty men.
Spare, Thou God of mercy, then!

Lord all-pitying, Jesu blest!
Grant them Thine eternal rest.

Amen.

INDEX.

PRINTED BY JAMES PARKER, CROWN-YARD, OXFORD.

9 783741 192807